THE QUEEN'S
YEOMAN

T.D. Raufson

Printed in the United States of America
First Printing, 2014
ISBN: 0988863537
ISBN-13: 978-0988863538

Twin Cedars Enterprises
twincedarsenterprises@gmail.com

Dedication

To Courtney who introduced me to these wonderful characters and this amazing world, partly in her mind and partly in mine.

Other Books By T.D. Raufson

Legacy of Magic Series
Legacy of Dragons: Emergence

Reviews for Legacy of Dragons Emergence

"A visionary masterpiece of sheer brilliance..." - Lucinda - Published on Amazon.com

"It is a book that will make the reader imagine the wonders of a world where magic is real."

Contents

Chapter 1 - Saundra's New Slippers

I t was not all that long ago, or very far away at all, when a young girl was last approached by a unicorn for help. Before we get too deep into those details, though, first let me tell you a little bit about why this particular girl was even approached by the unicorn.

Saundra was not all that different from all the other girls who attended Challenger's Academy. She was blonde, just like about half of the other girls in her sixth grade class. She was shorter than the average girl at the school—although she never noticed, and really neither did the unicorn. It wasn't her blue eyes, or her glasses, or any other feature you might at first think would attract a unicorn to a young girl. Saundra was not all that familiar with horses who are, after all, close cousins to unicorns. No, none of these things attracted the unicorn to her. Instead, the unicorn was attracted to her because of a simple pair of slippers.

Before I tell you the tale of Saundra's first meeting with the unicorn, which is where you would think this story should start, I want to tell you more about the slippers.

About a year before Saundra met the unicorn, her grandmother had died after several months in a hospital near her home in the small town of Henderson. Henderson was a two hour drive north of Saundra's home town in Sterling, and each month her mother, father, and older sister would drive up to visit her grandmother. Saundra was not fond of the trip because she could only see her grandmother for a few minutes at the beginning of their visit. Then she had to sit in the waiting room with her older sister, Kelly, for the rest of the day. But, like most girls her age, she found ways to make the waiting entertaining.

The hospital was mostly gray. The floors were gray tile speckled with black and white flakes. The walls were gray from the ceiling down to a wooden rail that surrounded the room at the same height as Saundra's shoulder. A gray kind of yellow filled the rest of the wall below the rail. The furniture was not gray; it was blue, but it might as well have been gray. There were large square containers spread around the waiting room that held all sorts of gray-green plants. Amongst all of that gray, Saundra would wait for their parents with her older sister.

She made the best of the situation because of her grandmother. As far back as Saundra could remember, her grandmother had told her wondrous tales about the kingdom and the people who filled it. Those tales occupied her mind and brought the gray, unimaginative canvas that surrounded her to life while she waited.

Most times, she would pretend the waiting room was the queen's court where all of the queen's subjects came to request help from her or her champions, the Queen's Yeomen. Saundra always wanted to be one of those heroes. She wanted to journey across the kingdom to face the evils and the dragon that caused them. She wanted to bring peace to the kingdom, but she had never been able to really imagine herself just right, and a Queen's Yeoman had to be just right.

While sitting among the subjects, their tales would fill her mind. She never had to try hard to know what each subject wanted. Occasionally, when they were really interesting, she would share their stories with Kelly and quickly remember why waiting with her was so hard.

"Kelly, look," Saundra said as she thrust her hand and index finger out at the newest family that had just sat down across from them. They were upside down to her. She was lying with her feet above her and pointing toward the ceiling on the back of the blue chair. Her head was flopped over the edge and her pony-tail brushed the floor.

Kelly looked up from her book with the agitated look that was so often associated with Saundra's interruptions. She pressed her own glasses up her nose, grabbed Saundra's hand to stop her from pointing, and nearly growled her response.

"What?"

"It's the miller. He's brought his entire family to the queen because the dragon has blocked the stream. He's unable to make meal. He can't face the dragon alone, but he doesn't want to let her down. That's the fifth family here to report that the dragon has moved

3

against the queen's lands. Something very bad is up in the kingdom."

"Stop that and sit up." Kelly's frown deepened.

She was three years older than Saundra, and their parents always left her in charge when they had to wait anywhere. Saundra didn't mind, but she worried that her sister had lost her imagination somewhere. She didn't talk about the kingdom anymore. She found her books and their stories more interesting. Saundra never understood why she needed those books when she had the kingdom to entertain her.

To enforce her order, Kelly squeezed Saundra's hand and pulled at her wrist as if she could lift Saundra up by it.

"Ouch, that hurts."

"Sit up."

Saundra did as she was told, not because she wanted to but because it was the fastest way to stop the pain. She scowled at her sister as she sat up but continued her tale. "Someday, the queen will ask me to take on that dragon. Someday, I'll find a way to rid the kingdom of his evil."

Every time Saundra tried to tell her about the kingdom, Kelly would scowl or smirk. It was like she was ashamed of ever being in the kingdom at all. By now, Kelly could have been a Queen's Yeoman for sure, but ever since she had started middle school she had hid in her fantasy books instead of sharing stories of the kingdom like she had when they were younger. The waiting room made Kelly want to escape the reality of their grandmother's sickness, but escaping in the world she had created for them seemed to make Kelly feel worse.

"Grow up. They're not here to see the queen.

You're so silly. Mom's right, there's no way she could leave you down here alone. So I have to stay with you. The least you can do is behave."

Saundra frowned at her sister's moping and returned to watching the comings and goings of the queen's court until it was time for them to leave.

Normally they would spend most of the day in the waiting room, but on this day their parents returned before Kelly had a chance to become more agitated. When Saundra saw them coming she jumped from her seat and ran to greet them. Even with the shortened day, she had collected several odd tales to share with her father on the trip home. She looked forward to the way her father listened and asked questions when she shared them. She knew he would have so many questions for her because all of her new stories were so dire and hopeless. It would have been depressing if she was not sure that the Queen's Yeomen were on their way to deal with each problem. The kingdom would be safe again soon. By the time they made it home, her father would be satisfied that everything was under control.

Saundra's smile faltered as their parents came closer. She stopped at the end of the row of chairs.

There was something worse than a dragon on her mother's mind. Tears were running down her face. She rarely cried. When she did, she never let tears run down her face.

Her father had his arm around her shoulder, and he looked like the miller had looked when he arrived to tell the queen of the dragon's actions. When they reached the chairs, their mother couldn't speak to them. She turned away and sobbed into a ficus tree at the end of the row. Kelly joined Saundra and waited to hear what was troubling them. Saundra felt a knot form in her stomach.

Their father kneeled down in front of them. Saundra could see the stress of what was on his mind drawing his normally smiling eyes down into a frown. He sighed as he resolved himself to tell them.

"Listen, guys. You know we've always been up front with you two about things."

Saundra watched his face and could see the smile struggling with the sorrow he felt. She suddenly realized what he had to tell them. There was no other possible outcome from such a dark day in the queen's court.

"The dragon killed her, didn't he? The dragon killed the queen."

Her father's head tilted a little to look at her. Kelly pulled away, stomped her foot at Saundra, and backed away from the bad news.

"Shut up!" Kelly shouted, drawing the attention of several of the other visitors to the waiting room. Ignoring their stares she ran into her mother's arms, where she collapsed against her shoulder. They cried together in huge sobs as their mother stroked her hair.

Realizing that she really understood what was going on, her father gave Saundra a sympathetic frown and placed his hand comfortingly on the side of her head.

"Yes, the queen is dead, sweetheart." He stretched his arms out toward her as much to comfort himself as to help her, and Saundra accepted the hug. She felt the tears come, and she buried her face in her father's shoulder and cried. He lifted her from the ground and carried her out to the car. On the way out, he whispered consolations to her, but Saundra knew that her grandmother, the queen, had died fighting for the kingdom. In the end, when her people had needed her the most, she had faced the dragon.

By the time they were in the car, Saundra had reconciled her sadness with pride that her queen had sacrificed herself to keep the dragon at bay. Although she was sad, very sad, that the queen had died, Saundra was suddenly more concerned about the kingdom. Who would take the queen's place? Someone had to continue to fight the dragon or the kingdom would fall. Could the Queen's Yeomen hold it off? Were there other heroes who could help? How could she help them?

The questions she fought with as they pulled out of the hospital parking lot distracted her. She didn't realize they were not going home. Instead, she struggled with the question of who would succeed her grandmother and lead the kingdom to victory. Their mother, who was the next in line, should take over, but Saundra was quite sure she had no imagination at all. Her father, who surely could understand the importance of what had just happened, was a member of the royal family by marriage. He could never take the crown.

All of these serious thoughts, unusual for a girl her age, filled her head and kept her distracted until she suddenly realized things were not as she expected. Panic at the difference filled her mind. She suddenly could not imagine why they would be going anywhere but home.

"Where are we going?" she asked with more agitation than she normally felt.

"We're following your grandfather home," her

father said softly.

"Why?"

Kelly harrumphed in the corner of her seat and scowled at her as if she had just asked the dumbest question possible.

"We have to help him arrange the funeral," her mother answered, "and we need to clean up a little. Most of the family will be coming here for the funeral and the house needs to be ready."

"Oh," she replied. The answer calmed her panic.

With the emergency averted, she chose to watch the trees go by for a while as her mind continued to struggle with who would take over the throne. She hoped the kingdom could withstand the onslaught until a new queen could be selected.

Of course, no one else in the family understood what she did, not even her father who listened to her stories had really understood what she meant when she called their grandmother the queen. Kelly had abandoned the kingdom for her books. Her mother had, as far as Saundra knew, never visited it. Despair for the kingdom overcame her, and she cried quietly against the window as they drove to their grandfather's house. Saundra had no idea of the future ahead of her. She had no idea that she was about to find a secret in the attic of their grandparents' house that would lead her to a meeting with a unicorn that would decide the future of the very kingdom she was so worried about.

~~~

The old house was really too big for her grandparents.

They spent most of their time on the first floor, slept on the second floor, and used the third floor and attic as storage. Whenever Kelly and Saundra had visited their grandparents before, Saundra always found her way to the rooms on the third floor because that was where she could dig through all kinds of boxes and imagine all kinds of adventures.

From the moment the car pulled into the driveway, Saundra knew she needed to disappear. She needed to get out of the way before she made her mother angry. She needed to get to the third floor.

"Girls," her mother said in that way that said she had something very important to share. "I'm not looking forward to what we're going to have to do. We had not planned on being here this long, so your father is going back to the house to get our things. I'm sorry you're going to have to spend your fall break up here. I don't want you two fighting all the time. I need for you to get along while we're here. Can you both do that?"

Kelly looked at their mother like she had stabbed her. To her, any argument was Saundra's fault. Before Kelly could make her point, Saundra spoke.

"Don't worry, mommy, I'll do my best to be good while we're here."

Unable to resist, Kelly snorted loudly at her words. Their mother pulled herself around the seat so she could look directly into Kelly's eyes.

"Young lady. That is exactly the thing I'm talking about. You're as much at fault as she is most times. I need for both of you to try your best."

Kelly nodded, shocked that she had been fooled by her sister and more shocked that her mother had been so cross with her. She was not used to being scolded. Saundra wanted to gloat, but she had meant what she said and knew that her mother would see her gloating as bad behavior. So, she waited until her mother was sure they both understood the instructions and turned around to talk to their father before she stuck her tongue out at Kelly.

Her older sibling pointed at her and started to call their mother. Saundra watched as the words formed in her sister's mouth. She watched as she then swallowed them. They had both been around long enough to know that any interruption so close to a warning like that would cause serious punishment. It would not matter that she was telling the truth. Kelly flopped back against the seat and adjusted her glasses.

After they hugged and kissed their father, all three of them walked into the very still, old house. Kelly was still moping, but Saundra had decided that her first instinct was the best way to keep from getting into trouble. If she stayed as far away from Kelly as she could, she would be fine. She could already tell that Kelly was not going to be far from their mother, so the best place for Saundra was where she wanted to be anyway. As soon as they were through the door and she had hugged her very sad grandfather, she was running up the stairs heading toward adventure. The fact that this was not all that different from normal didn't really impress her, but her grandfather actually laughed.

"Nothing really changes with that one," he said as she disappeared onto the second story landing. "It is good to see that at least one of us knows how to get on with their life."

"Be careful—not that she can hear me now anyway," her mother said as she was halfway up the third story stairs.

Kelly said nothing.

With each step she could feel her freedom growing. She could sense that the solution to her problems would be found at the top of the stairs. The sorrow and sadness she felt would be healed among the discarded pieces of life that made up her adventures in the kingdom. There would be a solution up there.

At the top of the staircase she slipped around the top rail and into the long hall that split the top floor down the middle. Five doors lined the hallway, three on one side and two on the other. She knew the center door was the bathroom that had not ever worked as far as she knew. The other four were rooms that were fairly packed with boxes. Although they tried to keep the hallway clear, there were several dusty, old chairs, a love seat, a clock that occasionally tick-tocked but didn't today, a card table stacked with magazines that were old and brown, and a full-height standing mirror.

Like an old friend she had not seen in a long time, she rushed to the mirror and stood directly in front of it. There was an odd line than ran down the middle of the glass that looked like a huge nose. If Saundra listed all of the pieces of furniture she played with, this mirror would be at the very top of the list, and now she knew why she had raced up there. If anyone could help her solve such a difficult problem, the mirror could. With her hands on her hips, she asked it exactly who was the fairest in the land.

"Your sister, of course," it answered with a chuckle.

She enjoyed the mirror's humor. It never failed to

make her laugh.

"What do you wish to play today? There is so much here to choose from."

"I need your help. The kingdom needs your help. What are we to do? How do we save the kingdom?"

The mirror's expression never changed, but Saundra was an expert at knowing when it was serious and when it was playful. In this situation it was very serious.

"Today, you should play. The kingdom is not lost. Although the queen is gone, there will be a tomorrow. There is too much to the kingdom for this to destroy it. Today, let's play. What shall we play today?"

"I don't know." Saundra raised her hands up to her head on either side, twisted her feet, and shifted her weight to the opposite side. The mirror had convinced her that her heart needed to play. She tossed her long hair over her shoulder to brush it as she primped in the mirror, and then looked around at the clutter in the long hallway. "What do you suggest?"

"Because I get to play too, I suggest dress up."

"Really, already?"

"You know it's my favorite game, and it has been so long."

"Okay, just for you. Because it's been so long since we've been here, we'll go straight to the best."

If the mirror had had any other facial features other than a giant nose, she knew she would have seen a smile.

"Be right back."

"There's a new box in the first room," the mirror suggested.

Saundra followed his instructions to the largest

box she had ever seen. To get into it, she would have to stand on a chair, and she would probably never reach the bottom of it.

"How'm I supposed to get anything out of it?"

"There's a chair against the wall."

"Yeah, but it's so deep I can't reach too far into it."

"So? I really want to know what's in it."

"All right, give me a minute."

Saundra pushed a stack of newspapers off the chair and dragged it noisily across the floor to the edge of the box. When she stood on the chair, the box came up to her waist. She had no idea how anyone could move such a large box. The flaps on the box were open like most of the other boxes, and she flung them aside to see what was in it.

A long bar ran across the top of the box. It was like she was looking down into a closet. She felt like she had just opened a chest full of jewels. There were all sorts of clothes in the box.

"Well, what's in it?" the mirror asked, a little agitated at having to wait.

"We hit the jackpot." She smiled back over her shoulder at the mirror in the hall, even though it couldn't see her where she was standing.

"Let me see," it cried.

Saundra moved some of the clothes aside and pulled a particularly nice blue and green dress from the bar. When she had as much control of the hanger as she could hope for, she pulled, expecting the garment to resist. It came loose so easily that the chair tilted over, and she and the dress toppled toward the ground. Luckily there was another box behind her that she fell into; otherwise, her promise to be good would have tumbled down around her ears. As it was, she knew the promise could not possibly survive the day, but she did want to try.

The cardboard top of the box gave way and she fell into a jumble of shoes. The dress settled on top of her. For just a moment she lay among the shoes with the dress draped over her.

That was when she realized why the dress had come out so easily. Most of the clothes she played in while she hid on the third floor were her grandmother's or grandfather's old clothes, and they were very big on her. This dress was only a little larger than what she normally wore.

"Are you okay?" the mirror asked.

"Yeah. Whose clothes are these?"

"I don't know. I didn't even know they were clothes."

With a little effort she pulled herself out of the box of shoes. As she did several odd shoes poured out of the collapsed side of the box with her. All of the shoes in the box were close to her size.

She set the dress on a box next to her, stepped out of the pile of shoes that had poured out around her, and picked up the chair. When she climbed back up and looked into the deep box she could see that all of the clothes were for a girl pretty close to her age. A big smile spread across her face. She jumped down from the chair and ran into the hallway, grabbing the dress as she ran.

When she reached the mirror, she pulled the hanger up under her neck and spun around, holding the dress in front of her.

"Look at what I found. It's a princess dress."

She continued to spin around in front of the

mirror.

"It's magnificent."

"I know, and it's almost my size," she said as she stopped spinning and kicked off her shoes. Leaving her clothes on, she slipped the blue and green dress over her head. She spun around one more time in front of the mirror, letting the slightly longer than knee-length dress spin out around her. With a giggle she ran back into the room.

"Now, I just need some princess slippers."

She dove into the pile of shoes, tossing aside leather mary-janes and other cloth shoes until she found exactly what she needed. Lying on the floor on either side of the pile was an elegant pair of silk green slippers with toes encrusted with emeralds. Grabbing one shoe in each hand, she jumped back through the door and flopped down in front of the mirror.

"Don't you just love these?" she squealed.

Without looking, she pushed each slipper onto the closest foot. Both feet complained about the shoes and she crossed her eyes at them before she realized each was on the wrong foot. When she switched them out and stood up, there was no doubt Saundra had found her princess slippers. Her toes wiggled in the open hole at the front of the shoes and her heart skipped in time with them. She was so happy with the dress and shoes that she started spinning again.

"Where did you find those?"

Her sister's voice slammed into her happy moment, and she stopped spinning to face her. Kelly was standing at the top of the staircase staring at her.

"In a box."

Kelly shook her head and pointed down the stairs. "Mom wants you downstairs."

"What for?"

"Ask her, she told me to come get you."

"You know what she wants. You're just being mean."

"So?"

Saundra decided that she wasn't going to fight with her sister. The happiness of finding the slippers was better than the possible trouble she could cause if she got Kelly agitated and caused an argument in front of their mother. There was something serious about the way she had warned them in the car. If she messed up now, she might not be able to come back up when she was done with whatever her mother wanted.

"Okay."

Her lack of argument irritated Kelly, who expected a fight.

"You can't wear that downstairs."

"Why not?"

"Because, we can't drag stuff out of the attic."

"They never said that."

"To you. They know you can't listen."

Saundra felt her desire to show her sister bubble up, and she started to walk past her in the dress and slippers. She stopped instead and pulled the dress over her head and laid it on the loveseat where she could find it when she came back.

"The shoes, too."

Saundra thought about taking them off, but they felt so good. She didn't want to leave them behind.

"No," was all she said before she ran past her sister and down the stairs.

Kelly followed her down the staircase. Their combined footsteps on the old wooden stairs created a rumble like a freight train that spilled into the front foyer ahead of them. Saundra reached the foyer first, where she slid to a stop in front of her mother.

"What are those?" her mother said, pointing at the green cloth slippers on her feet that were covered with not-so-complete patches of glitter.

"They're my princess slippers," she answered.

"They're hideous."

"I told her to leave them up there," Kelly chimed in, expecting a smile of praise but instead received a frown.

"Take those back upstairs…" Saundra started to turn back around when her mother caught her by the shoulder, "after dinner." She smiled down at her for the first time that day. "Go get cleaned up and get to the kitchen before the food gets cold."

Saundra grinned back and then raced away to get ready to eat. Kelly stood and stared at them both because she was not aware of how important those slippers were. Over the next week, while her parents helped their grandfather get through the funeral, Saundra hardly ever took them off while she spent most of her time on the third floor. Until the day of the funeral when she had to be in the same room with Kelly, she had avoided any fights. Interestingly, she also had to wear her black leather mary-janes that day too. Her mother was not too angry that they had finally had an argument and just let it go after she separated them into two different rooms downstairs.

They stayed a few more days after the funeral, and during those days Saundra met someone else on the third floor.

Chapter 2 – Visitor on the Third Floor

M ost people don't like to hang around after a funeral, but Saundra's Aunt Ellen was not most people. She decided that Saundra's mother needed help and was determined to be the one to provide it. To Saundra, spending time with Aunt Ellen was not as fun as a trip to the dentist. At least when she left the dentist, they gave her a lollipop.

The morning after the funeral Aunt Ellen started helping by herding Saundra and Kelly out of the kitchen immediately after breakfast. She didn't want them out of the kitchen for any real reason. She just wanted them out of the kitchen. For the first time in several days, Saundra and Kelly agreed on something.

"She's a little pushy today," Kelly said as they were almost out of earshot.

Saundra looked up at her to make sure it was really her sister that had said anything so close to an adult. She was usually very careful to avoid irritating them.

"Yep, Mommy says that she's trying to make up for not being here since grandma got sick."

For a moment they wandered into the front room of the house as a team. Saundra took their shared agitation as an indication that Kelly might be softening a little.

"Do you want to play dress up with me?"

Kelly thought about it before she answered. "No. Thanks, though. I think I'm just going to read while I have a chance."

Saundra shrugged. "Okay, you can always come up later. I'm sure we can have fun then, too."

Kelly actually smiled at her as they walked up to the second floor, where she climbed up on her bed to read. Saundra was okay with Kelly's choice because she had not been able to talk to the mirror in a few days because of the guests and the funeral. She really wanted to get back to their game.

"See ya. Come up later if you want."

Kelly smiled over the top of her book and shook her head without really looking away from the page.

Saundra shrugged and raced for the stairs. She had taken the slippers back upstairs like she had been told and had not seen them in a few days. She really hoped they were still hanging on the mirror where she had left them, but there was no way to know who else had been in the attic. She only had a few days left before she had to go back to school, and she wanted to have all sorts of stories to share with her friends when she got back.

At the top of the stairs she grabbed the rail and swung herself around to face the hallway and the mirror. Her dress was waiting on the loveseat, exactly where she had left it. She started to rush to it, but the slippers that should have been hanging from the mirror and weren't stopped her.

Saundra dropped to the floor and crossed her legs while still staring at the place where she had hung them. She reached out and dragged the dress to her from the loveseat and squeezed it into a tight hug while twisting back and forth. In her mind she was trying to figure out what happened.

"Where did they go?" she asked the mirror that never asked the first question.

"I don't know. For some reason, I could not see when they were taken, but I'm sure they were taken."

Saundra thought about the mirror's comments for a moment. She dropped her head into her hands and rested her elbows on her knees while she thought about what that meant.

"You mean, someone took them at night?"

"I can see at night as well as I can see during the day."

"Hmmm." Saundra pondered some more and then stood up. She was angry and wanted her slippers back. She had only been able to wear them for a little while. She turned from the mirror and stomped down the stairs. At the landing on the second floor she continued to pound each step until she was standing in the door looking at Kelly.

If Kelly heard her ponderous approach, she gave no sign of it. "Where are they?" Saundra asked, refusing to be put off of her search

Kelly finally looked up from her book, eyebrows squeezed closer together. Her chin jutted out at Saundra. "Where are what?"

"You know."

"I don't."

"Yes, you do. It had to be you. Who else would take them? You never want me to have any fun."

Kelly sat up and set her book aside. "What are you talking about? Can't you find your slippers?"

With a look that was very close to concern, Kelly slipped off the bed and stood up. Saundra, convinced more than before that she had taken them, did not quite take her actions as concern. Instead, she saw her sister standing and gloating. In Saundra's mind her slippers were nearby, possibly even behind Kelly's back.

"Give. Them. Back." Saundra stomped her foot with each word and shoved her fists into her hips at the end to emphasize that she was serious.

"I. Don't. Have. Them." Kelly matched Saundra's tone and stance.

Saundra was forced, for a moment, to listen to her sister. She considered her position but refused to give up.

"Who else would have taken them?"

"Who else would want them?" Kelly asked as if the slippers were covered in mud or something worse.

Saundra didn't have an answer. Instead, she stared at her sister and Kelly stared back.

"What in the world is with all that stomping? What are you girls doing?"

Saundra froze. A bolt of fear rushed up her back. She had no idea why Aunt Ellen had taken that moment to come upstairs. The last thing Saundra needed was an adult mediating a fight over a silly pair of dress-up slippers. They never understood why it was important, and they always took Kelly's side.

"We're just playing, Aunt Ellen," Kelly answered in a playful and joking way to cover the fight. They still needed to be on their best behavior.

"It sounds like it. Saundra, go on and play by yourself. I think it's time for Kelly to learn a little bit about being mommy's little helper."

Out of the corner of her eye Saundra noticed how Kelly glanced at the book on the bed and then back up at Aunt Ellen. She didn't look happy to be included in whatever plan Aunt Ellen had in mind.

"What are we going to do?" Kelly had to ask, and she tried to sound interested even though Saundra knew she was anything but. In that flash of time, Saundra felt sorry for her sister and started to argue that she had wanted to play with her, but she didn't say anything.

"Grandpa's moving to Toliver. We're going to help pack up some stuff for him and get ready to close the house up for a while." Aunt Ellen smiled at them both. "Come on, give your Aunt a hand with this, Kelly. I never get to see you anymore."

Kelly abandoned any hope of reading and nodded to her aunt before following her out of the room. Saundra was left standing in the room without her slippers and with the sudden news that her grandfather was moving so far away that she would probably never see him again. As soon as she settled that surprise into her mind, she slowly dragged herself back up to the third floor.

This time, at the top of the stairs, she walked over to the mirror with the weight of her sudden revelation.

"So who is the fairest in the land?"

"Your sister, of course," the mirror laughed, but this time it laughed alone. "What's wrong? I'm sure we will find your slippers."

"It's not that. Grandpa's moving out. He's moving to Toliver with Aunt Ellen."

"Hmmm. I see," the mirror said. "I'm touched that you're so concerned that you might not see me again."

Saundra had not thought about that possibility. She considered what else the news could mean. She might never see anything else that was in the house. She could not control the tear that dripped off of her nose.

"No need to cry," the mirror said.

"Why not, there's no end to the changes. First we lost the queen, now Grandpa is moving. I'm tired of change."

"Well, what if you could take me with you?"

Saundra looked up at the tall mirror and shook her head. "There's no way. Mom would never let me take you with me."

"What if I was smaller? Do you have a purse?"

"No. Yes. Kinda." Saundra was not sure of anything just then.

"You can always carry me with you in your purse, if you have one."

Saundra looked up at the old glass front of the mirror and the long streak on its backing that made it look like a nose.

"Really?"

"Of course you can."

"How?"

"I'll need your help, and you'll need your slippers. You're going to have to go on a quest for them, it seems."

Saundra sat up straighter in front of the mirror and smiled through the tears that dried on her face.

"I always like a quest," she sniffed.

"I know, but this one could be dangerous because whoever took your slippers probably doesn't want you to find them. Why else would they want to keep me from seeing them take the slippers?"

Saundra looked around the old hallway and found what she would need for her adventure. First she collected an old backpack that smelled far better than it looked. In the backpack she stuffed an old flashlight, a length of cord, and a red cape from the box of clothes. She wrapped an old canvas belt around her waist and shoved a really old director's baton into it. The last item she needed was a brass fire poker. She took it in both hands and looked at herself in the mirror.

Saundra looked just like the hero she wanted to be, except for her slippers. Her axe would protect her from any monsters she might run into. The wand in her belt would give her all of the magical help she might need. In the backpack she had her lantern and her cloak. All that remained was food for the journey.

"Be right back," she said to the mirror before she walked to the stairs. Below her all she could hear was the quiet of the house. Her mother, sister, and aunt would be on the bottom floor, but that was where the food was, too. She walked slowly to the second floor, listening. At the top of the stairs to the first floor, she could hear her mother and aunt talking in the living room. They were discussing pictures on the mantel over the fireplace and her grandmother's mantel clock. As they argued politely about who was going to take the clock home, Saundra walked quietly into the kitchen.

There were a few leftover biscuits from breakfast

in the covered bowl on the table. Saundra slipped her hand under the cloth and took three of them. Her mother was explaining how important the old clock was to her, and Ellen was hinting without saying how likely it was that the clock would be broken in a year.

Saundra stopped in front of the refrigerator. She wanted to tell her aunt that she should just say what she meant. Everyone knew she was saying Saundra or her sister would break the stupid clock.

Trying to remain quiet, Saundra opened the refrigerator. On the middle shelf she found a box of single-serving cheese sticks. She grabbed three quickly and let the door close. The conversation in the living room had stopped, and someone was walking toward the kitchen.

Her heart skipped, and she refused to breathe. Saundra was not sure why she was suddenly scared, but she tiptoed out of the kitchen quickly.

As soon as she was near the stairs, she quietly bounded up toward the second floor. Her mother didn't care if she snacked a little between meals, but she would have to explain why she was taking so much food if they caught her. When she reached the second floor, she didn't stop until she reached the top floor.

"So, you are a thief," a strange voice accused her.

Standing next to the mirror with his left hand resting on the hilt of a long but thin sword was a boy about Saundra's age. He was wearing dark green leggings and shirt. Over his shirt he wore a waist length black cape with a hood that was pulled over his head. The hood did not allow her to see his face. From the knee down he wore black boots with equally dark buckles. Saundra had the impression that he was mostly shadow.

"No," was all she could think of to say.

"I've been watching you."

"So."

"And, you're looking for a pair of green slippers that were hanging on this mirror yesterday."

"Maybe."

He laughed at her. "This is my room. You can't lie to me about what's in it. I know where your slippers are."

"And, you're going to help me find them?"

"No. You must find them on your own."

"Why?"

"So you may become a Queen's Yeoman. You've proven that you can steal. Now you have to prove that you have the other skills you'll need."

Saundra could not deny the thrill that his words caused, but she controlled herself.

"Why would I want to be a Queen's Yeoman?"

"Perhaps you don't. Maybe you don't even know what I'm offering you," the boy said, "but the slippers are your key in, if you want in. I think you want in."

Of course she knew what a yeoman was. She had imagined stories where she traveled the entire kingdom on the order of the queen. She had vanquished evil in her name, hoping someday to attract her attention and be invited to join that royal corps. The boy's cape slipped off of his left hand and exposed the signet that only yeomen wore on their left pinky finger. It was proof that he was who he said.

"Why now? I've always wanted to help the queen, but she's dead."

"She is, and that is when the yeomen have to be

on guard the most. Without her guidance and until the new queen is found, we must protect the kingdom against the evil that wants to take it over. We're all that stands between the kingdom and the dragon."

"He dammed up the miller's stream."

"That's just the beginning. He sent an agent after your slippers."

"Why would he want them? My mother says they're just junk."

"To her, they are. To almost everyone else they probably are, but to you they are the most beautiful dance slippers you have ever found. If you need them to be silent boots for sneaking into a protected lair, they will be that for you as well. Because you found them, they are your key into the ranks of the Queen's Yeoman. If you don't recover them, you will never be a yeoman. But it will be far worse if they fall into the hands of the dragon, and his agent has them now."

Saundra thought of her sister and grew angry.

She had them.

She was working for the dragon.

Saundra was sure of it.

"Why?"

"Because he controlled those slippers once before, and he came close to overcoming the kingdom completely."

"He's killed the queen already, how much more does he need?"

"The queen is not the key to the magic that protects this kingdom. To take it over, he has to control or destroy the yeomen. He came close, long ago, to controlling a magic more powerful than the yeomen. The queen guides what happens here, but, without us, the kingdom would fall."

Saundra inhaled sharply. She could not let the dragon win this fight. Now she had two reasons to find the slippers. She had to find a way to take the mirror with her, and she had to become a Queen's Yeoman. She could not let the dragon destroy the kingdom.

"Find those slippers, Saundra. But, don't delay too long. If you wait too long, they'll be gone, and you'll never find them again. They're your key to becoming a yeoman."

Saundra nodded and started to ask the young boy what his name was, but he wrapped his cape around his body and stepped behind the mirror as a noise from the stairs caught her attention.

"Put that stuff down and come down for lunch," her sister growled from the edge of the stairs. "Aunt Ellen has made us grilled cheese sandwiches and tomato soup."

Saundra looked around the room for the yeoman who had just been with her. There was no sign he had ever been in the hallway.

Saundra was not a fan of grilled cheese, but she was hungry. What she didn't know was that she would soon learn who had taken her slippers. In the kitchen with her lunch, Saundra would meet the dragon's agent.

Chapter 3 – The Dragon's Agent

W hen Saundra reached the bottom of the stairs, she was still thinking about the mysterious boy and his odd assignment. She was so lost in her own thoughts about him and the promise of being a yeoman that she didn't see the slippers sitting on the table until she was in her chair. As she sat down, the slender baton she had stuffed in her belt poked her, and she slid it out onto the table. When she placed it carefully next to her napkin, she saw them out of the corner of her eye.

The sparkling green shoes were sitting at the far end of the table on top of a stack of newspapers, as if someone had collected them in a stack to be put away.

With the unbridled excitement of her age, she shoved her chair back from the table, causing it to tip over and slam into the floor. Everyone in the kitchen looked at the toppled chair to make sure she was okay, but she was on the other end of the table collecting the slippers in her arms.

"You found them!" she shouted and everyone who had been looking at the chair was now staring at her.

"Saundra! Put those down—Pick up your chair—Sit down, and eat your lunch." Kelly was shaking her head while their mother was angrily towering over the table.

Interpreting the instructions in her own way, Saundra slipped the shoes under her arm, walked over to the fallen chair, and tried to lift it off the floor with her one free hand. She tried twice but could not get the chair up without dropping the slippers, and she refused to let them go.

Kelly moved in her chair to stand and help her, but Ellen was next to her before anyone else could move. Their eyes met as she reached down to help Saundra with the chair, and something in her eyes scared her. Smiling at her aunt as if she was thankful for the help, Saundra shifted to pick up her side. Instead of grabbing the chair, Ellen reached over and pulled the slippers out from under her arm.

As they slipped from her grasp, Saundra reached to grab them back and dropped her side of the chair. The chair pounded on the floor again, and Ellen shook her head without saying a word. She pulled the slippers completely out of Saundra's reach.

When Saundra couldn't reach them, she looked up at the table and saw the end of her wand. She could stop this if she could just reach it. Her hand moved and as if her aunt knew what she was after, Ellen's hip bumped her as she walked back to her seat. Saundra sat down hard onto the floor. The shock of having her goal in her hands and having it ripped from her stunned her nearly as much as having the culprit be her own aunt. She looked up at her mother and sister, who were now standing over her. Kelly was reaching to help her up. Her mother was reaching for the chair, but all Saundra could see was everyone trying to keep her from reaching the slippers.

The next few moments for Saundra moved by slowly.

Ellen sat down in her seat at the end of the table.

Her mother righted her chair.

Kelly helped her up into it.

Ellen placed the slippers back on the stack of papers.

Her mother placed a bowl of soup and a plate with a sandwich on it in front of her.

When her mother finally sat down and Ellen was patting the slippers, Saundra could suddenly smell the soup and sandwich. The pungent aroma of the tomatoes shocked her and made her stomach react. For a moment she thought she was going to be sick.

"Saundra? Are you alright?" her mother asked with a concerned look on her face.

"I'm not sure… I don't feel so good."

"Come now, child. You're just hungry." Ellen countered her mother's concern. "She's fine, Jen. There's nothing to be concerned about. She'll feel better once she has some food in her. She's been up in that dust and mildew all morning. You should consider keeping her downstairs this afternoon."

Her mother nodded, looking at Saundra as if she was broken and her aunt knew how to fix her.

Saundra fought the nausea back and scooped up a spoon full of soup. When she had swallowed the acidic sweet mixture and ripped off a crumbling piece of the melted cheese and bread to force it down, she smiled up at her mother.

"I'm fine, see," she said to help her mother relax and forget her aunt's suggestion. As she scooped more soup into her mouth and struggled to keep it down, she stared at the shimmering shoes at the end of the table. How could she get them now? Why was Aunt Ellen protecting them so?

Saundra continued to eat her sandwich quietly while she struggled with the reality that she didn't want to believe. Her aunt was the dragon's agent. Earlier that same day she had believed her sister had taken the slippers, but there they were, and her aunt was guarding them. What was she going to do? Maybe she could cast a spell on her aunt to get them back.

She ate a few more bites while she decided just what she would need to cast the right spell. She looked down at the table and saw the wand again. That was a start, but she didn't have anything else to work with except the bowl of soup.

She considered the possible outcome of using tomato soup and decided it was worth a try. When everyone was looking at their own food, she picked up her wand from beside her napkin. The movement caught her mother's eye. Fear trickled down Saundra's back, but it was too late to stop. The web of the spell was already being spun.

She pointed the wand at her bowl and waved it in a circle just over the surface of the soup. With the little incantation running through her head she pointed the wand straight into the air and thought about getting the slippers from her aunt.

Her mother continued to watch her over her own

bowl. The others were eating quietly unaware of her actions. Saundra felt the fear melt away. Satisfied she had cast the spell as well as she could, she placed the wand back on the table, picked up her spoon, and ate a few more bites.

Her mother shook her head and turned back to her own food.

As the meal continued in awkward silence, Saundra was convinced the spell was not going to work—it was based on tomato soup, after all. When she was about to give up on it, Kelly spoke up from her own bowl.

"Aunt Ellen, where did you find those slippers? Saundra had been playing with them for days before the funeral. She couldn't find them this morning, and it really upset her."

Saundra looked over her half-eaten sandwich at her aunt, who placed her spoon delicately in her bowl. She didn't even react to the last part of Kelly's question.

"It's the most interesting thing," she said. "I had forgotten all about those slippers until the other day. I went upstairs to look around, you know, to see what we needed to move and what we needed to get rid of and there they were, hanging on that old full length mirror. So I took them down. I thought I might as well take them home with me."

Saundra's heart skipped a beat at the thought of Ellen taking the slippers. She was taking their grandfather away and ruining any chance she would have of ever being a yeoman. Saundra needed those slippers. If she couldn't finish this simple mission, they would never trust her with anything harder.

"But why are they so important? Why did you

even want them? Saundra really liked them. Maybe you could let her have them."

"Kelly." Their mother's scolding tone surprised Kelly a little, but she didn't stop.

"What? She just seems so aggressive about some old green slippers that she can't even wear. Saundra liked them so much. What's the big deal?" Kelly could get away with her tone because she was tired, but it was risky. Saundra felt her sandwich bubble around in her stomach a little as her no-conflict sister fought for her.

"Kelly, they're her slippers," their mother informed them. Saundra swallowed a spoon full of soup to avoid the noise she nearly couldn't stop. "They're not Saundra's."

"Oh," Kelly said when she realized she couldn't argue about that.

The table was silent for a few more bites. Then, for some reason Saundra never understood, Kelly took a chance she never thought her sister was capable of.

"Aunt Ellen, Saundra was really enjoying playing with your slippers. It really upset her this morning when they were gone. Would you mind at all if she—I mean—could she…play with them after lunch? It may make the packing go easier…if she's not in our way."

Saundra stopped eating the last of her soup and stared at her sister. For a moment she didn't know if she was more amazed or insulted. For just an instant she thought she saw a smile on her mother's face, but when she looked back it was gone and there was no proof it was ever there.

"You know, El. Kelly's right. We really need to

focus this afternoon or we'll never get everything down here packed for dad. The stuff upstairs can wait until this summer."

Saundra watched and wondered if they were really helping her or if she was just imagining it all. She looked down at the wand and shook her head. She would never underestimate the power of tomato soup again.

Ellen looked unsure of her answer. She chewed on her lip a little. After she had taken a few moments, she finally answered, "Of course she can play with them. I certainly enjoyed them for years. Just be careful with them."

Saundra nodded her acceptance of the rules as she scooped the last bite of soup out of her bowl. A few more bites and lunch would be over, but she took her time so the power of the spell and the decision could clear the air a little. She could not wait to show them to the yeoman upstairs. This would fulfill her quest. This would make her a Queen's Yeoman. It was all she could do to sit still until everyone had finished their lunch.

After a few minutes of silence, Kelly pushed her empty bowl aside and looked up at their mother.

"Mom, I'd like to go read a few minutes before we get back to packing."

"Why don't you both go play a little while? I need to talk to your aunt."

Kelly stood up and motioned to Saundra to come with her, but Saundra had something else on her mind. She stood up, plucked up her wand, stuck it in her belt again, and walked over to her aunt's chair.

"Thank you, for letting me play with your slippers, Aunt Ellen. I know they must mean a lot to you."

Saundra was not an impolite girl. Her mother had taught her manners, and she intended to demonstrate that to her aunt.

"You're welcome, child." She smiled down at Saundra with a very unconvincing smile and pushed the slippers toward her. Saundra carefully collected them and left the kitchen behind her sister. Just outside the doorway, they both dived to the side where they could not be seen and waited to hear whatever it was their mother wanted to talk to their aunt about.

Saundra stretched her head toward the kitchen. She couldn't hear anything, and she thought she might be too far away. Kelly shook her head at her and put a finger to her lips. Just as Saundra was about to give up on hearing anything, her mother spoke.

"El, what in the world was that about?"

"They're mine, Jen, and I want them."

"They're a worn-out pair of slippers that you can't wear anymore. They're a piece of our childhood you would never have even remembered if Saundra had not found them upstairs."

Saundra nodded aggressively and Kelly shook her head with her finger over her lips.

"I did so remember them."

"You did not. And, then to take them and make a show of them like that. You sent both my daughters into a tizzy. Intentionally."

"Well, you should be doing something about that one's imagination. She's not going to make it in the real world if you keep letting her fill her mind with nonsense."

Saundra scowled and put both fists on her hips.

"I think I'll handle raising my own children if you

don't mind."

"I don't mind at all, if you'll just do it."

"Who are you to judge her. El, you used to run all over the house in those slippers going on about the kingdom and the dragon, and you want to talk to me about my child's imagination."

"I didn't think you remembered that," Ellen said quietly into her bowl.

"How could I forget it? Why do you think I'm asking you to let Saundra keep the slippers?"

Saundra raised both hands in the air and danced around in a circle. Kelly grabbed her and pulled her against the wall.

Silence followed their mother's last statement.

Neither girl took or released a breath.

If they were caught listening they would be in serious trouble. The spell would break and she would have to give the slippers back.

Saundra was not going to be able to hold her breath much longer.

"You're just going to take it all from me, aren't you?" Aunt Ellen responded.

"Really, El. You're taking dad so far away from me that I may never see him again, and you're upset about a clock and a pair of ratty, old, sentimental slippers. I'm glad my daughters can't see their aunt demonstrate her love for her own sister."

Realizing that the conversation was getting serious, Kelly pointed toward the staircase. Saundra grasped the slippers and the handle of her wand while calling on whatever was left of her tomato soup to help her mother.

Both sisters turned away from the kitchen door and tip-toed toward the stairs. They nearly crawled up them waiting for a tattle-tale creak to give them away. On hands and knees, they both rolled onto the second floor landing. Saundra stared up at the intricate crown molding and could not wait to get up to the third floor.

Kelly, who had rolled to a sitting position and was looking at her sister, suddenly stood up and walked toward their room.

"Kelly," Saundra called to her as she was almost through the door.

"Yeah," she responded and looked back at her.

"Thanks, for… you know."

"Yeah, I know."

"If you want to come up later and play, you know where I'll be."

"Yeah, I know."

This time Kelly closed her door as a sign that she was serious about being left alone. In that moment, Saundra felt a little sorry for her sister and how she had accused her of taking the slippers.

Saundra rolled back over, pushed herself up off the floor, and left her sister with her book. Although she was anxious to get upstairs, she walked up the stairs slowly, thinking about what had just happened. She had her slippers, for now. Her mother was trying to get her aunt to let her keep them, and her sister was not so bad after all. Saundra was not sure what to think of the changes.

"Nice trick with the spell," the yeoman said to her as she turned to enter the hallway on the third floor. "You may make it as a yeoman yet."

Although she was surprised to see the young boy standing in the corner at the top of the stairs, she was glad he was there. His presence meant she had succeeded and she was going to be a Queen's Yeoman. But she pretended she wasn't sure what he was talking about.

"What spell?"

"The spell you cast to get the slippers. You must be pretty powerful. That's okay; we need an enchantress as much as we need crafty little acrobats like me."

"So, I'm in?"

"In what?"

"I'm a yeoman?"

"Sure you are. But that's not something to really celebrate. It's dangerous doing what we do. We're resisting a powerful dragon that wants to take control of the kingdom."

"I guess." She wouldn't let herself feel bad about becoming a yeoman at that moment.

"Well, I'll see you around."

"You're leaving?"

"Your mom and aunt are talking about closing the place up. I'm going to have to find somewhere else to stay."

"Will I see you again?"

"Of course you will."

"When?"

"Sometime soon. Anyway, I've got to go." The boy turned to walk back into the stacks of history and disappear when Saundra reached out and grabbed his arm. He turned to scowl at her with a questioning look.

"What do I call you? What's your name?"

"Call me Max."

With nothing more to say, he jumped up onto a box next to the mirror and disappeared behind a stack of Christmas decorations.

"Well, isn't that strange?" Saundra asked herself.

"Very," the mirror answered.

Saundra, who had almost had enough surprises for one day, jumped when the mirror answered her. Then, she remembered that the mirror was going to help her take him with her when she left, and she smiled.

"I have my slippers. How can I take you with me?"

"Do you have a small mirror?"

She thought about that for a minute and remembered that her sister carried a small mirror in her purse.

"Just a second," she said and ran down the stairs to borrow a mirror.

Saundra didn't explain to her sister why she needed the mirror, and Kelly gladly surrendered it to protect her precious few remaining minutes of reading time.

Saundra bounded up the steps again and listened carefully to the floor mirror explain the magical spell that would transfer him. When they were done, Saundra looked at small rectangle of glass with a crooked scratch running down it and knew she would never be giving the mirror back to her sister.

That was the last time the sisters, either set of them, were in that house together. Saundra and Kelly never went back, and their mother handled the last arrangements for the house over the summer while the daughters were at summer camp.

On the trip back home, Saundra—with the mirror Kelly didn't really want back because of the nose-shaped scratch that ran down the length of it, a director's baton that she used as a wand, a red cape with powers yet to be discovered, a lantern, and her travelling backpack—told her sister all about becoming a Queen's Yeoman, whether she wanted to hear the tales or not.

Now remember, it was the slippers that attracted the unicorn to Saundra. So, there's more to this tale to come, and it all takes place after summer camp, after the next school year started, and after Saundra met her new friend, Max, who transferred in at the beginning of that same year.

Chapter 4 – Max

By the time Saundra made it through the first week of the new school year, she had learned that not everyone shared her very detailed imagination. Summer camp had been an interesting challenge. She had hoped she could enjoy a few weeks outdoors with friends who understood her. Instead she had learned to keep her stories about the queen and the kingdom to herself. After the first few days of school, when everything looked just like the year before and Saundra was starting to relax among her peers, a new student arrived in her classroom and set everything on its ear.

It was not unusual for new students to start at her school.

It was not really unusual for a student to start late. But, for that new student to be in Saundra's class, and for that new student to be named Max, was unusual. It was almost too unusual for Saundra to accept.

She tried for a few days to ignore the similarities to the yeoman guide she had met over fall break nearly a year before. Because she had not seen his face, or his hands, or any part of him, really, Saundra had no way of knowing if this new Max was the same Max. But, by the second week, she could no longer resist. In the hall, outside the cafeteria, Saundra stopped Max and the collection of friends he had quickly attracted.

"When are you going to quit pretending?"

"Excuse me?" Max asked with a surprised look on his face.

Saundra fumbled a bit at his response because she was sure, after several days of convincing herself, that Max was ignoring her and waiting to see how long she was going to take to approach him. This was not the response she had imagined.

"We—we met last fall, in Henderson," she said, struggling to find a way to remind him of the conversation on the third floor of her grandfather's house.

"No, we didn't." His abrupt and less than polite response made her very sure that she had been mistaken, and the laughter from his cloud of followers advised her that it was wise to leave it alone for now. There was no reason to act out one of her recurring school nightmares. She let the laughing cluster walk past her.

Saundra was not the type of girl to give up on an idea though, and she was sure this was the same boy. After she was over the embarrassment of being laughed at by his friends and once she realized that she didn't really care what they thought of her, she was even more convinced that she really was right about Max. Her obsession with him had even made her the recipient of a popular children's tune. Amanda hummed the familiar tune about her and Max in a tree somewhere while they were sitting out front waiting for their parents. Saundra didn't feel that she deserved the song since all she was doing was following him around and watching him wait for his ride. Anyway, he was a boy.

"Stop it," she snapped at her friend.

"Tell me I'm wrong."

Amanda's father was a lawyer who encouraged his daughter to stand her ground, make her logic clear, and dare anyone to prove her wrong. Some days Saundra found it fun, as her friend picked on the boys in their class who deserved the flogging. Suddenly, being the defendant made her rethink her appreciation of that skill.

"I know that I know him. We met while I was at my Grandmother's funeral."

"So what is he doing here?" Amanda pressed and walked around Saundra, making her dark curls dance as she skipped to the other side between her and Max. "Why doesn't he know you?"

Saundra shrugged as Amanda moved to the other side and sat down next to her to deliver the next question while she looked into Saundra's eyes.

"Why are you staring at him like he's a poster on your wall?"

"I'm trying to see what he would look like if he was wearing—Never mind, he's lying."

"Ooh, sensitive," she smiled and whirled away from Saundra to come to rest against a nearby pole. She pointed her index finger at her. "You'll have to prove he's lying. You can't just say it."

Sandra closed her notebook where she had not

been doing her homework and stood up from the short wall that held the flowers edging the sidewalk in front of the single story academy. Without sharing things Saundra would rather keep to herself, there was no way she could tell Amanda why she was stalking Max. It wouldn't make any difference even if she did tell her.

The next morning Amanda would have a rather wicked rumor circulating the classroom about Saundra and Max. There was nothing she could do to stop that now. Saundra gave up and ignored both Amanda and Max as she waited the last few minutes until her mother arrived to pick her up.

Kelly, who was now in middle school, attended band practice after school and would be home later, so Saundra spent the afternoon thinking about the yeoman Max and how she would get him to admit he knew her.

If someone asked Saundra why it bothered her so much that he didn't seem to know her, she could not give them a good answer.

She was convinced it was him.

She intended to prove it.

By the end of the night she had decided that for the first time since they had come home with her, the slippers were coming to school with her. There was no way he could deny that he remembered the slippers.

The next morning, as she choked down her dry toast and half a grapefruit before she rushed out to ride with her father to school, her mother came downstairs to see her off.

"Saundra, is everything all right at school?"

Saundra swallowed the last bite of dry toast hard

and wished she had not.

"Fine," she answered with a high pitched squeak that drew her mother's attention closer.

"What's wrong? Are you getting sick?"

"Nope. You surprised me. I swallowed my toast wrong," she croaked out a response while rushing to the kitchen for a glass of milk, and that was when her mother saw the slippers.

Saundra filled her glass, washed down the rough toast, and returned to the living room before anyone said anything. She should have known something was wrong, but still had no idea as she threw her backpack over her shoulder and turned to face the door.

Her mother was standing with her arms crossed and a sour look on her face. The look shifted from Saundra's father, who was suddenly looking at Saundra's feet, to her. Saundra waited for the reason for her mother's look to become clear.

"You didn't really think you were going to wear those to school, did you?" she asked as if the answer should be no.

Saundra looked at her outfit.

She was not seeing the reason she should answer no.

She raised both hands to her side.

She was wearing her tan uniform skirt.

She was wearing a clean white shirt.

She was even wearing a belt. She forgot that most often.

She looked up at her mother confused but wanting to answer correctly.

"Those slippers, Saundra." She actually pointed at her feet. "You can't wear them to school."

"Why not?"

"First, it's not allowed. It's not part of the uniform. But beyond that, I'm not allowing you out of the house with those on. They look like you found them on the side of the road."

Saundra looked down at the slippers. They sparkled back at her in the morning light. They were the only thing Max was going to remember, and she needed him to remember her. For a moment she wished Amanda was there to defend her choice, but, remembering the last time Amanda had argued with her mother, Saundra decided that would have only made this worse. She didn't move, and her mother grew more upset.

"Saundra, listen to me. You're going to make your father late. Take those off now and put on your tennis shoes."

She dared not resist her mother's clear instructions.

She had before.

She would not again.

She slipped the shoes off, picked them up, and walked to the closet to find the shoes she wore to school every day. As she walked by, her mother pulled the slippers from her. Saundra reached for them, but her mother gave her the infamous look that warned her she was very close to being in a lot of trouble.

"They will be in your room when you get home." Without another word her mother walked up the stairs and left Saundra to figure out what she would do now to get Max to admit he was her yeoman guide.

"Come on, kiddo," Kelly said and put an arm around her. "You can tell me about it on the way to school." They both walked to the car together. Saundra didn't even flinch at her sister's comforting arm around her shoulders.

Although Kelly had been true to her word and had listened to her explain why she needed the slippers, it had done nothing to improve Saundra's mood. When she met Amanda that morning, she was not ready to face her argumentative friend. If the strange tale of her fondness for Max was not already circulating, it would be by lunch.

After lunch, which Saundra had taken as far away from Max and Amanda as she could, she chose to continue to hide. It would seem like a hard thing to do on a playground full of children, but every playground had places no children went.

There were dark foreboding places that came with stories that older siblings shared. There were places so far away from the teachers and monitors that, although everyone wanted to go to them, they were often used as dares when someone really wanted to put you on the spot. But there were also places so charged with history, real or imagined, that no student ventured there more than once.

On the odd day when Saundra's imagination was not up to the challenge, she hid in the open by visiting Nancy's Perch. That was what everyone called the very top of the wooden climbing tower on the back side of the playground. Every level below was always filled with children, but the very top and the rope used to climb down from it were never used.

Nancy Gilroy had fallen from the top a few years before. Her fall had been surprising enough without the gory tales of what happened after the fall.

Some said that the fall had damaged her face and

because of the deformity she hid in a tower room at her grandmother's house. Others agreed that the fall had actually killed her, and the school was just keeping that a secret.

It was not true that Nancy had died from the fall.

It was true that Nancy had not come back to the school after the fall.

It was true that she was living with her grandmother, but not because she was deformed and hiding in a tower.

Saundra's mother had explained to her that Nancy was going to another school and it had nothing to do with the accident, but the way the story still circulated reminded Saundra why the truth was not always the tale everyone shared. In this case, the fiction was close enough to the truth that it made the stories even more exciting.

In one of the more sensational tales of why she fell, the tower was guarded by an evil wizard, and he had thrown her out of the tower as punishment for interfering with his experiments on children. That tale was enough to keep everyone away from the top of the tower, making it one of the most peaceful places on the playground.

In her attempt to avoid Max, this was her final mistake.

"Everyone tells me this spot is haunted."

Saundra felt her heart jump again like she had when he had snuck up on her at the old house, and she grabbed the frame of the opening where she was sitting to keep herself from tumbling down after Nancy.

"I asked several others why you would feel safe to sit up here in the spot where poor Nancy was thrown from. Most of them had no answer. The answers I did receive were very interesting."

"What are you doing up here, Max?" She scowled at him as she regained control.

"I came up to talk to you."

"Why?"

"You seem upset."

"You almost made me jump out of this tower. Yes, I'm a little upset."

"Not about that. You've been avoiding me all day."

"So? You don't know who I am. Why do you suddenly care?"

"You're right. I don't, but apparently your friends think..."

"I know what they think. So—what—you came up here to give them something to talk about? Proof?"

"No, I came up here because since you stopped me in the hall yesterday, you seem to be upset that I didn't know you. I'm sorry if my reaction was mean. You surprised me in front of everyone. What was I supposed to say?"

Saundra suddenly wished Amanda was with her, but she would never brave the dangers of Nancy's Perch.

"I didn't mean to surprise you. I just..."

"Yes you did. You waited for me to come out into the hall where you could surprise me. So, who do you think I am?"

Now she felt trapped. If he really was Max, her Max, then he already knew what she didn't want to tell him. If he wasn't and she told him about the queen and the yeomen, he would probably make fun of her.

"Never mind, Max. We've never met before," she said and launched herself off of the perch toward the ground.

It was a move she had practiced many times.

As she fell forward slightly she reached out and grabbed the rope. It was how you were supposed to get down from the tower, and she had never been afraid of it or the supposed magical guardian. Although the under-used rope bit into her hands a little more than she liked, she refused to show any reaction as she lowered herself to the ground and walked back toward the teachers and the entrance to the classrooms. Luckily the bell rang before she made it to the door. She didn't want to turn back and face him after making such a successful exit.

The rest of the day she refused to even look at him and kept her head stuffed into a book, a storage cube, or her backpack. When the last subject was behind her, Saundra collected her homework notebook from her named slot, stuffed it into her backpack, and rushed out the door to wait for her mother. That day her luck held, and her mother was waiting for her when she reached the sidewalk.

She rushed to the car, opened the back door, and jumped into the seat. Her mother looked back over the headrest at her.

"Everything all right?"

"Yep. No problem."

"How was your day?"

"Okay, I guess."

"Homework?"

"Some."

"We have to go to a meeting with Kelly tonight. What is it so we can get it done?"

"Let me look," Saundra said as she pulled out her homework notebook to look up the assignment.

Stuck into the notebook between pages was a note she had not seen before. She pulled out the half sheet of notebook paper and started to read it.

Saundra,

You're right. I know you. I need to talk to you, but we can't talk in the open. Don't go back to the perch. Follow my lead tomorrow.

Max :)

"Well?"

"What? Oh." Saundra shuffled to the page and looked at the homework list. "Ugh, It's math and spelling."

"Well, get started when we get home so you're not up too late."

Saundra closed the notebook and read the note again. She had been right. He did know her, and he wanted to talk to her. She felt happy for the first time in days. She was right.

Max had warned Saundra that being a Queen's Yeoman was not everything she imagined it would be. What she didn't realize as she rejoiced over being right was that very soon they would be faced with the danger that yeomen were meant to face. Before the unicorn could introduce her to her ultimate challenge, the two yeomen would first have to face the Guardian.

Chapter 5 – A Meeting with The Guardian

As Saundra walked into the classroom the next morning, she was not sure what to expect from Max. His note was not clear about what he planned to do, and Saundra did not like the tone of his warning.

She reached into her backpack and pulled out her homework notebook, without the note, so she could turn in the assignments from the night before just as Max ran into the room. He was obviously out of breath and reached out clumsily to grab her arm before she inserted her folder into her slot.

"What is your problem this morning?" she asked as she tugged at his grip on her arm.

"Can't—breathe. Ran—front—late—wait," was all he could gasp out between deep breaths.

"The bell is about to ring, and I need to turn this in," she reminded him as she tried again to insert her folder into the slot.

He shook his head and motioned for her to step

away from the crowd of other students forming at the box.

She pulled her notebook and the precious homework that would most assuredly determine her future back from the slot. When the folder was out, Max relaxed a little and pulled her to a spot in the corner of the room where they could have a quick, quiet conversation.

He reached for her notebook. She yanked it away from him and stuck it in the safest place she could reach, behind her back.

"I'm not going to let you copy my homework. There's no time anyway."

Max shook his head, took a final breath that allowed him to speak again, and answered her accusation.

"I don't need to copy your homework, but you can't turn in your spelling. Not yet."

"What? Why?"

"What happens if you don't turn it in?"

"I have to finish it and turn it in after recess. I have to sit on the wall and finish it while everyone else is at recess."

"Right," he said as if he had made his point.

"So? Not happening." She moved to walk back to the box.

"So, I need to talk to you somewhere that we will not be overheard. No one comes near the wall. We will be alone and uninterrupted."

"You can't expect me to get in trouble like this. My mother…"

"…will never know. Why do you think they make you do it at recess?"

"To punish me for not doing my homework,

which I did, by the way."

"No, to get you to do it. The punishment is just a plus. They won't tell your mom if you finish it at recess."

"How do you know that?"

"Do you really think this is the first time I've done something like this?"

Saundra looked at him. She remembered the boy she had met over fall break. Quickly, she decided he knew what he was doing. With trembling fingers she brought the folder back from behind her back and removed the spelling paper from the sacred storage her mother had checked less than an hour before.

"If my mother finds out about this…"

"You'll kill me. I know, I've heard that one before."

"Oh, you'll only wish I had killed you if my mother gets involved in this."

"Don't lose that. I don't really want to do homework at recess today."

She smirked at him and closed the notebook. Together they walked over to the box and released their homework, without their spelling, into the unrecoverable slot.

In about an hour Saundra would reap the fruits of her deception. It always came early. Miss Fowler always checked the folders first thing and had meetings with anyone who had trouble with their homework during their first work period.

As class started, she tried to focus on what Miss Fowler was telling them, but couldn't. Her hand itched. The agitated butterflies in her stomach promised to introduce the entire class to her breakfast. Twice she scowled across the room at Max for putting her in this situation. Each time he made some hand motion that made no sense to her. By the time the instruction session for their morning assignment was over, Saundra's head was on her desk. She had no idea what she was supposed to do.

When the instructions came to take out their workbooks and start the assignment on the board, Saundra was not even sure which book to use, but her suffering was not to last much longer.

"Saundra."

At the calling of her name, her head popped off of her desk, and she sat straight up in her chair. The movement conspired with the butterflies, but she kept her stomach as calm as she could.

"Yes, Miss Fowler?" she answered with the standard questioning response.

"Can I see you up here, please?"

First? She was first? Why did she have to be the first one called? She nearly cried as she replied, "Yes, ma'am."

She stood and walked as straight as she could to her teacher's desk at the front of the room. She knew that the other students, her friends, were supposed to be working. They were not supposed to be watching her, but she was sure they were staring at her, waiting to hear every word that passed between her and Miss Fowler.

At the edge of the teacher's tall desk, Saundra stopped and looked down at her own plain white tennis shoes. She suddenly wished she had her slippers with her. She could use the support. She didn't look back at Max, even though she wanted to.

"Saundra, are you all right?"

The question shocked her.

"I'm sorry, what did you ask, Miss Fowler?"

The concerned look on her teacher's face was nothing like the condemning scowl she expected.

"I said, are you all right? You seem very distracted, and you did not turn in your spelling homework from last night."

Saundra felt the dizziness building in her head as she tried to answer the question, but the words never made it out. Her breakfast, however, did.

Miss Fowler showed exactly how agile she was by gathering her garbage can from under her desk in time and getting Saundra out of the classroom before any other students joined the chorus.

Saundra was not really sure what happened next. She walked out of the classroom and down the hall to the nurse's office in a fog. When her head was clear again she was laying on the narrow bed in the nurse's office with a cool towel folded across her eyes.

"Your mother is on her way." Those were the first words she heard from the nurse, and she wished the mattress beneath her would open up and swallow her. That was exactly what she didn't want to happen. Now she would know she had not turned in her homework, even though she had done it. How could she ever explain that? Max made me do it. First of all, how did she explain who Max even was?

She growled something unintelligible and shrunk into the pillow.

"I know. I hate being sick, too. Were you feeling okay when you came in this morning?"

Saundra nodded into her chest but refused to speak.

"How is she?" The voice at the door was Miss Fowler's, but Saundra refused to look at her. Not only had she deceived her about her homework, she had thrown up in her garbage can.

"She just woke up," the nurse answered with a surprisingly chipper response. "Whatever made her sick wore her out as well."

"Hmmm. Saundra, listen. Your mom is on the way here now. We called her because you were sick. Do you remember what happened?"

Saundra nodded again.

"Don't worry about your spelling homework. Max found it on the floor near the door and brought it to me when I returned to the room. I hope you feel better."

She nodded that she had heard her but still didn't look at her. She couldn't face her. She made up her mind, as she started to recover, that she would pay Max back for putting her in this spot, even if he was her yeoman guide. She made up her mind that day that he would pay for embarrassing her in front of her friends. She wasn't really aware of it, but that was the moment she had started thinking about how to get her slippers to school. Before, she had wanted to show him who she was, but now, hidden in the back of her mind, she wanted to teach him who she was.

The rest of that day she spent in bed. She felt better after a few hours and actually enjoyed some time with her mother. At lunch, over another bowl of soup, chicken noodle this time, the seed she had planted in the nurse's office bloomed and she took her first step.

"Mommy, I know you don't want me to wear my slippers to school."

Her introduction caused her mother to put down her spoon. Saundra felt the sudden resistance but forged ahead anyway.

"But, if I only wore them on the playground, could I take them with me? Can I put them in my backpack? Please?"

Her mother sat and looked at her for a little while. Saundra had not really been aware that she was even thinking about that question when she decided to ask it. She had been enjoying her soup and time with her mother. The question had rushed from the back corner of her subconscious where she had been working on it and out of her mouth. She watched her mother struggle with the question as she tried to answer.

"Well…"

She ate a few bites of her sandwich and then returned to her soup.

After a few spoons full of soup, she drew up another one and then answered.

"Yes," she said decisively over her spoon.

Saundra looked at her, somewhat amazed.

"Only for recess, though. I figure, if the boys can take cars and stuff to school for recess, you can take your slippers."

Her mother smiled at her.

"Now finish your soup. Do you think you might feel up to doing your homework tonight? I don't want you to get behind."

Saundra nodded into her soup and smiled back.

"Yes, ma'am. I want to be ready for school tomorrow, too."

Although Saundra knew her mother was thinking of her grades, she had other ideas about what being ready for school meant. Those she kept to herself.

The next morning, when class started, Saundra was

in her seat, having already turned in all of her homework, and ignored Max as he tried to talk to her.

If he thought she had been mad at him after their first conversation in the hall, he was in for a surprise. She avoided him for the entire day. As she walked onto the playground wearing her shiny, green slippers, she was fixed on finding him and finding out what game he was playing.

She followed his bobbing head across the open spaces until she was sure he was heading to the tower before she took off after him. When she stepped off of the sidewalk, her slippers changed into low suede boots that rolled down just above her ankles. They were much better for walking through the forest.

In her mind, the playground transformed into a dark forest, and the tower extended above the trees, watching over the long plateau in all directions. A trail led through the trees up to the open gate of the keep.

Saundra set off to follow Max. He had warned her in his note to stay away from the keep and Nancy's Perch, but he was heading straight to it. She wanted to know why.

The gate was unguarded, and the grounds around the keep were shaded by tall, knurly trees. The trees in the kingdom were still covered in multicolored leaves. She stepped into the foreboding darkness of the keep's shadow and shivered from the sudden impression of being alone. As she approached the base of the tower, she could see the double doors at its base were open. She walked up the stone stairs and into the main room at its base. It was filled with tapestries that showed what Saundra assumed were yeomen engaged in heroic feats to defend the kingdom. Above a giant fireplace in the opposite wall was a frame that, at one time, had held a painting.

The portrait had been burned out of the frame. Strips of charred canvas still hung from the wooden frame. Black soot stained the wall and ceiling high overhead where the fire had burned quickly, destroying only the image within the frame.

Remembering that she was following Max, Saundra turned away from the destroyed painting and started climbing the stairs that crawled broadly out of the main hall and up the outer wall of the keep. Arrow slits allowed some light into the dark tower, but the meager beams were unable to fight their way through the gloom that filled it.

At each floor she paused to look for Max. It was a large place to search but she could not ignore the feeling that he was heading to its peak. He was on his way to Nancy's Perch. Saundra had visited the tower to find peace, but in the kingdom the tower was a much different place.

Every floor contained a different type of room. Each room was guarded by stationary suits of armor that seemed to watch her as she walked up the stairs to the next level.

Each floor became a little brighter as she ascended out of the forest and more light could penetrate the darkness.

Each floor grew more interesting as she passed an armory, a training room, an alchemist's laboratory, and finally the sun-soaked top floor.

At the top of the stairs, Saundra found an open floor surrounded by battlements. It was the defended ramparts that looked out onto the plateau. It commanded a view like none other. Sitting in the center of the top floor was a giant siege engine prepared to rain all sorts of alchemical destruction down on invaders that climbed to the top of the plateau. It looked like the engine could reach the very edges of the land the view commanded.

The catapult was manned by six suits of armor and was set on wheels that were recessed into a groove in the floor. There were two suits positioned to turn the siege engine to face any direction. Two more were poised to load it. The final two manning the catapult were standing ready to turn the crank that armed it.

Two more suits of armor stood guard at an opening on the far side of the battlements where a block and tackle was rigged to lift heavy cases of ammunition from the alchemist's lab below. When they were not recovering ammunition, they would act as lookouts for any encroaching army. None of them moved as she reached the top of the stairs.

Standing near this opening on the far side of the tower was a tall man with a clean-shaven young face. He wore a tight-fitting turban of muted greens and blues that complimented his loose-fitting top with voluminous sleeves and his baggy pants with matching legs. He carried a rod in his left hand with two metal claws hooking out of the bottom and a crystal spike thrusting out of the top. The center of the rod, between the spike and the claws, was wrapped in a leather casing that was studded with metal and laced up with black sinew.

At his waist, the tall man wore a burgundy sash that wrapped around him and hung down his left side to his knees. Suspended from it he wore a wickedly curved sword on the left side, and a matching dagger was stuffed into the sash on his right side.

Max was standing before this striking guardian. He

seemed very relaxed to be facing such a powerful looking man, and he was not at all uncomfortable considering his warning for her to stay away. Saundra wondered what he was up to, and she was determined to find out.

She slipped onto the roof of the tower on her hands and knees and stole between two stationary suits of armor which were poised to crank the arming lever on the catapult. From where she knelt she could see the man and hear his conversation with Max, but unless they looked toward her, they could not see her.

"…she's struggling with everything too much," the master of the tower stated to Max.

"Some, yes, but she's very capable."

"Ah, he defends her. And how has she won your admiration so easily?"

"Don't be fooled. It's not admiration, but more like appreciation. She drew me into her imagination from my own dream. I was in a hospital bed recovering from having my tonsils out. She drew me into her grandmother's house."

"What you describe is very difficult to do. Only the queen and the dragon can pull others into the kingdom."

"I never said she pulled me into the kingdom. She pulled me to where she was in the kingdom. That's different. But, I'm still concerned that she's dangerous."

"Like the last one?"

"Regrettably, yes, or perhaps worse."

"You think she's a threat to us?"

"This is a pivotal time. We can't afford to lose the ground we've gained. Her power is a threat. After being pulled into her imagination, I have no doubt of it."

"But, you helped her become a yeoman."

"And, how do you suggest I was supposed to stop her?"

"So, you plan to bring her to me to deal with then?"

"You dealt with the last one. She has never ventured into the kingdom again. She's obviously no longer a threat."

Saundra could not believe what she was hearing. She wondered who they were talking about. She didn't dare get any closer, but there was no need. She could hear well enough where she was. She did shift her hip to sit on the floor next to the suit of armor instead of staying on her knees.

The guardian shook his head and looked over his right shoulder at the opening in the battlements. He stroked his shaved chin and looked down at Max.

"Bring her to me, if you can convince her. I will expel her from the kingdom like I did the last one."

Saundra could feel the anger building in her, but she was not equipped to face the Guardian.

"You nearly killed the last one; can you try to be a little more careful with this one? There's no reason to kill them to keep them out of the kingdom."

"She gave me no choice. She came here to take it from me." He gripped at something beneath his blouse. "She was powerful, too. You stand here telling me your tales of power, but you didn't face her. If I had not done what I did, she would have destroyed my tower. I cannot surrender control of the plateau."

"Forgive me. I didn't mean to insult you. I cannot argue with your results. I'll bring her to you tomorrow."

"You still have to convince her to come before me. I've watched her sit on this very spot and never enter the kingdom."

Saundra sensed the conversation was ending, and she knew Max would see her when he left. She needed to think about what she had heard before she faced him again.

Slipping backward out of her hiding place among the armor, she stopped when she felt a tug on her right side. Her belt, the one she had not forgotten, snagged on the poleyn protecting the knee of the suit on her right. If she continued back she might tip it over and bring it down around her. She moved forward a little to try and pull free and realized she was really caught.

As quietly as she could, she turned to look at what was holding her. As she shifted the metal suit clanked, and her belt slipped free. The noise was not very loud, but it was enough to draw the Guardian's attention. She looked back up into his green eyes. He realized immediately that she had overheard them and acted.

Saundra saw him shift his left hand, but he was too far away to hit her with the rod. There was no way he could reach her before she made it to the stairs. Free from her snag, she turned to run just as his shout rang out.

"Stop her!"

She shook her head. Max couldn't catch her at this point. All she had to do was make the stairs and she would get away. She was two steps away when the suit of armor behind her moved, reached down, and grabbed her by the waist of her skirt. In her mind she cursed her belt again as she flew backward through the air toward the Guardian.

She had nothing with her but her slippers, so she felt unprepared to face the Guardian, who was reaching out to her with his rod. The claw at the end was poised to grab her, and there was no way for her to change directions. He was going to catch her. What was he going to do when he caught her?

Max said he had almost killed the last one. Did he mean Nancy? Was the Guardian why she had fallen from the top of the tower?

Her answer came too quickly as his rod grabbed her and propelled her toward the opening in the battlements. His redirection had turned her around and she was facing the opening as she flew toward it. There was nothing for her to grab. She had no weapon and the opening was now rushing at her.

She could see the ground beyond rushing toward her, and she could feel the hopelessness of her situation settling into her bones. Her eye caught sight of her savior. She had done it many times before on the tower on the playground, but it was not this high.

The thin line of the rope was racing toward her. He would never expect her to grab it. This had worked with Nancy. This is how he ran her off. He had to think it would work against Saundra.

She only had one chance. She reached as the rope was passing her and wrapped both hands around it. She felt the coarse cord bite into her hands. The heat of the rope burn almost forced her to let go. She was still moving so fast that she wondered if she was going to be able to slow down before she slammed into the ground.

When she was not sure she could hold on any longer, she jerked to a stop and hung from the rope.

Suddenly the world around her was a playground. She was hanging five feet off the ground.

Students on the tower were gaping at her. She had no idea what they had seen. Gingerly, she released her grip on the rope and lowered herself the remaining feet to the ground. Each arm-length of rope jarred her as she felt the blisters in each hand protest. When she was within her height from the ground, she released the rope and walked away from the tower. She didn't look back to see if Max was watching. She knew where he stood. He was not her ally. She could not trust him. She was alone.

She would not remain alone, however. Soon her greatest ally would appear and share with her the secret to saving the kingdom. Soon she would meet the unicorn and everything would be different.

Chapter 6 – The Unicorn's Quest

For the next two weeks, Saundra avoided both Max and the Guardian. The guardian was not a challenge; all she had to do was stay out of the tower. Max, on the other hand, was difficult.

Because he was in her class, he was always there. She had no choice but treat him worse than any other student in her class, and that still had not worked. Miss Fowler had even asked her, after one particularly bad day on the playground, if there was something wrong between her and Max.

It was getting to the point where her friends were resurfacing the rumors of her affection for Max. It was a way for them to explain her ignoring him and to tell her they were embarrassed by her. At the beginning of the third week, she was not sure she was going to be able to ignore him much longer.

That week they had a field trip to a local organic urban farm, and it would be impossible to avoid him like she had on the playground. So, before she left for school the morning of the trip, she made sure she was prepared. She was not taking chances with Max anymore.

She loaded her backpack with her lunch, permission slip, homework, slippers, wand, and cape. Although the farm was larger than the playground, there would be fewer students for her to hide among and more adults to force them together.

For the duration of her ride to school she had plotted different ways that Max could end up stuck at school where she wouldn't have to worry about him. She settled on the most likely. He could leave his permission slip at home or lose it. Then he would have to stay behind. She didn't care where he spent his time, so long as it was not near her. She spent several minutes envisioning the multitude of ways that he could lose or forget it.

By the time they were loading onto the bus, she had convinced herself that he had really forgotten his permission slip. When Max approached the line to board the bus, already late, he was fumbling through his backpack with a look of agitation. At one point he looked up from the search with a pained look of anger directed straight at her. She felt a pang of guilt but continued to watch. There was no way she had caused him to lose his permission slip.

"Max, I have to load the bus. Either find your permission slip now, or I will have to send you to the library for the rest of the day," Miss Fowler advised him loud enough that Saundra could hear.

Max redoubled his efforts. He began to pull out each book in his bag and leaf through the pages. Miss Fowler was losing her patience with the show, but she continued to wait. As Max grabbed his math book, Saundra gasped. That was the last place she had thought of him losing his permission slip.

When the slip fell out of the book and fluttered to the ground at Miss Fowler's feet, Saundra shivered. Max looked directly at her. His face was a confused combination of relief at finding the slip and anger. The anger morphed into his best I'll-show-her look. Saundra shivered again. As Max boarded the bus, she pulled her cape out of her bag and snugged it around her shoulders.

The old wool cape had been beautiful when it was new, but the years had not been kind. To Saundra, it was as nice as any sheer cape she could have worn, and it immediately chased off the draft that had been sneaking in around her. She closed her eyes and leaned her head against the window of the bus to wait.

"What'cha dreamin' about?" Max asked with a put-on drawl.

She kept her eyes closed and ignored him.

"You can choose to ignore me if you want, but it's an hour drive to the farm. Can you ignore me all the way there?"

She thought about the challenge and decided it was worth a try.

"Nice spell you cast on me this morning. How did you do that? How did you bring it out here, outside of the kingdom?"

She continued to struggle with ignoring him, but she had to admit that she was intrigued about why her wishing and dreaming about him losing his permission slip had actually come close to working. She quickly convinced herself that he was imagining things. Magic from the kingdom only existed in the kingdom.

"No one else has ever been able to affect someone else's view of the kingdom. But, not only can you affect other people in the kingdom, you can affect them out here."

"That's not possible," she replied, no longer able to ignore him. "And even if it is, it's no reason to kill me." She opened her eyes and looked at his surprised face.

"You weren't supposed to hear that. You aren't supposed to be able to get into my imagination without me including you."

"Don't blame me. You included me when you started plotting my death."

"I was not."

"The guardian was, and he seemed ready to act on his plans, too."

"You have this all wrong."

"Explain it to me," she said with a huff.

He looked at her knowing he was not going to be able to. She was sure she had won when he suddenly took a different tack.

"Where did your slippers come from?"

She refused to answer.

"It's important that I know."

"Why, so you can finish what you started?" She wanted to storm off and leave him where he was, but her worst nightmare of what could happen on the field trip was happening. She was trapped where she could not get away from him. "Leave me alone or I'm telling Miss Fowler you're bullying me."

He took her threat seriously and sat for a moment quietly. Then he came at her from another direction.

"How are you related to Nancy?"

"You mean, am I related to Nancy Gilroy?"

"No, I assume you're related. I want to know how."

"I'm not related to her at all."

"Hmm," he sighed and looked out the window at the trees slipping by.

She closed her eyes again and leaned against the window.

"You have to be related."

"Wrong. I don't have to be related. My mother knows her mother. They were in school together."

His face screwed up into a scowl, and he looked back out the window. When he had a moment to think he turned back around in his seat.

"Your aunt was the dragon's agent."

"You say. I think she just wanted her slippers back."

"So, they were her slippers."

Saundra frowned at how he got her to answer his first question anyway.

"Leave me alone."

"Saundra, this is important. It's important to the kingdom."

"I used to dream of being a champion for the queen and going on quests for her. I used to want so bad to be a Queen's Yeoman, but since the queen was killed by the dragon, everything's been bad. That's the same time you came along saying you were a Queen's Yeoman. That's the same time you started calling my aunt an agent of the dragon. I want my imagination back. I want you out of it. I really want the queen back. Leave me alone." She pulled the hood of the cape up and leaned her head against the window.

She had never covered her head with the hood of the cape. The entire bus was suddenly silent, and it scared her. She threw the hood back and looked around.

Noise from all around her slammed into her ears. Max was looking at her as if he had said something profound and was waiting for a response.

She slipped the hood up again and closed her eyes into the peaceful silence it provided. For the rest of the ride, she enjoyed the blessed silence and ignored Max. When the bus stopped, she slipped her hood off and listened to the instructions. Max stared at her, and she ignored him.

They were going on a tour of the farm, and then they would have an hour to explore while enjoying their provided lunch. Saundra was really looking forward to exploring the farm. It wasn't because she was really interested in farming. It was mostly because she was interested in exploring and this was a new place with new experiences awaiting her.

As the bus started to empty, she held her seat. She reached into her backpack and took out the slippers and her wand. Max was waiting on her, and she was not going to be unprepared when he was around ever again. She slipped on the shoes and stuck her wand into her belt before she stood up. When she finally exited the bus, Max stepped up behind her. She would have to lose him later, because she had no intention of being chased all over the farm. She thought about catching up with her friends but decided that dealing with their taunts about Max was worse than dealing with Max. Instead she found a place in the middle of the class and stayed there.

As she had wiggled through the crowd, Max had

stayed right with her. She knew their combined actions were feeding the rumor mill, because it was well known that if you hung around someone on a field trip, you must really like them. She groaned and resigned herself to not losing him until lunch.

She walked through the tour without speaking at all even though Max tried to start a few conversations. Through the tour she paid just enough attention to answer the questions that she knew would be waiting for them back at school. Then they reached the fenced in animal paddocks.

The central paddock was a large field enclosed in a three rail horse fence. The farm also had a stable, and they had released the horses into the field for the school's visit. Saundra walked over to the fence and draped her arms over the middle rail. The field was full of horses. Some were walking along the edge. A few were chasing one another across the grass. One horse, a very large white mare, was standing in the middle of the field looking at her. Its muscles rippled in the morning sun, and the glistening white hide seemed to shimmer like silk. It looked Saundra in the eyes and then tossed its head, disturbing a long silvery white mane that danced in the sunlight, creating multi-colored flashes like light passing through a prism.

Saundra looked around at her classmates who had joined her at the fence. They were all watching the horses, but none of them seemed at all shocked by the huge mare that was now walking toward them.

She reared up onto her hind legs and leaped into a gallop. In a very short distance it was at a full run with its head down aiming at Saundra. Its hooves pounded the ground.

It was still staring at her as it ran toward the fence.

Saundra shivered and abandoned her place on the fence. Stepping away from the other members of her class, she stumbled into Max, who reached out to catch her with a questioning look on his face. She was not comforted by his being there to save her and she pushed him away.

The horse surmounted the fence and the line of children to continue her pursuit of Saundra.

It landed on its front hooves, and the earth shook.

When its back hooves struck the ground with a thud like thunder, it turned after her. Saundra knew the horse was going to run her over. There was nowhere for her to go. Her classmates and teachers were reacting to the charging horse that had jumped the fence. Panic overcame them all.

Max, who looked less shocked by the charging horse, tried to reach her to pull her toward him, but she resisted him. Regaining some control, Saundra tried to jump out of the charging horse's way when it grabbed her in its mouth and tossed her like a sack of laundry over its back. She landed roughly around its neck and instinctively grabbed onto her mane to avoid falling off the other side and being trampled.

Saundra could not help but scream as the horse carried her away toward the woods, and no one could stop it.

"Stop screaming," it said to her.

She swallowed her last scream. Shock kept her from asking it why it talked to her, or even how it could talk at all. Unable to voice a response or think of anything, Saundra lay on its neck, gripped its glossy white mane, and held on as it charged into the woods on the opposite side of the farm.

When it broke through the outer edge of the woods, it slowed to a trot. Saundra found the new pace easier to handle and not as terrifying. She sat up a little but refused to release the death grip she had on its mane.

"It is good to see those slippers again," it said to her over its shoulder as it looked back at her.

Saundra was still not sure how to react to a talking horse. She looked into the single eye looking back at her.

"Don't be silly, girl. Horses can't talk," it said as if it was reading her mind. "Pull your hood up."

Still not sure what else to do, she pulled her hood over her head.

The forest before them changed.

A path cut wide enough for carriages appeared. The trees draped over them like a tunnel carved from the forest. Through breaks in the tree coverage, she could see what looked like a castle on top of a distant hill.

The real world was gone. They were in the kingdom.

"What's happening? How did you do that," Saundra asked.

"I didn't. I've been waiting for you. Like I said, it has been a while since I've seen those slippers."

"Why have you been waiting for me? What does this have to do with my slippers?"

"I've been waiting for you because I need your help. The slippers are how I knew someone who could help had finally arrived."

"Why would a horse need my help?"

"First, like I told you. Horses can't talk."

"I know that, but you're talking to me."

"Which means?"

Saundra looked at the horse. She looked into the eye that was looking back at her. In that single eye she felt an ancient wisdom. She could see tales unimagined beyond the golden flecks. Her coat was glistening and well cared for, but she had a wild look to her that was different than other animals Saundra had seen. The white of her coat was so shiny that it looked almost silver. A small patch of off-white fur, shaped like a diamond, sat between her eyes on her forehead. If Saundra had not been so close, the blaze would have been invisible.

"You're not a horse," Saundra answered.

"That's right, I'm not a horse. You're a smart girl. You are a Queen's Yeoman after all."

"I guess."

"What do you mean?"

"There was no ceremony. I'm not sure it's official, and I think I've made them mad."

"Really? How?"

Saundra suddenly wondered why it mattered. "I don't know. I just think they're mad at me."

"But you're wearing the slippers. You can hear me. You were able to bring us here. You're a Queen's Yeoman, and you can help me."

"I guess. It depends on what you need. I'm not sure what all I can do."

"If I'm not a horse, what do you think I am?"

Saundra knew the answer before she even asked the question. She had avoided it because she didn't dare hope she was talking to a real one, and it didn't have a horn. The blaze looked like a place where a horn would go. She wondered if the horn was just invisible so she could hide among the other horses.

"You're a unicorn."

"That was a very good guess."

"But, where's your horn?"

"Well, aren't you smart and observant? You do get right to the problem. A young girl, charmed by a dragon, came into the kingdom and took it."

"How is that possible?" Saundra asked. She had never heard tales of taking a unicorn's horn.

"She used powerful magic to take it. Then somehow she sneaked it out of the kingdom and hid it where I can't find it. The dragon's hold on her was broken before she could deliver the horn; otherwise, the kingdom would be very different. I need for you to help me find it."

"How? I don't know anything about where your horn is."

"The girl who used to wear those slippers knows where it is. She hid it."

Saundra felt like the unicorn had stabbed her in the chest. If Aunt Ellen had hidden the horn, that meant she had stolen it from the unicorn.

Saundra didn't want to believe her aunt was able to do what the unicorn said she did.

"You don't believe me."

"I don't know."

"I do. She hid the horn somewhere outside of the kingdom. I can't go beyond the borders to find it. I can't find her, but you can. You can find my horn and bring it back to me."

"I don't …"

"Right, you don't know," the unicorn repeated her earlier answer for her. "I can fix the kingdom if I have my horn. I can make it all right again."

Saundra caught a glimpse of something slip behind

a tree for just an instant. She sensed that she was being followed. The unicorn paused as she sensed Saundra's agitation.

"What is it?"

"We're not alone."

"Where?"

"Behind us. To the right."

"I can't do anything to help you. I'm very limited without my horn. That's why I needed your help to get us here together."

Saundra slipped off of the unicorn's back and stepped away from her.

"You're invisible," the unicorn told her. "Whoever is following us can only see me."

"Really?"

"That's one of the powers that cape has in the kingdom."

Saundra didn't say anything else as she walked toward the tree. She pulled her wand from her belt and pointed it out in front of her.

Quietly, she walked around the tree until she could see Max. He was cloaked like she had seen him that first day. He was very hard to see in the shadow of the tree. She pointed her wand at him, but as she prepared the spell in her head he turned and struck at her with his sword. The sharp blade nicked her nose as she fell back from his wild swing. Blood trickled from the gash and ran down to the tip of her nose.

He followed her footsteps as she moved out of the range of his sword arm.

The unicorn charged the tree where Max was still hiding and reared up to attack her assailant. Her front hooves slammed into the bark, chipping chunks out before coming down hard just behind Max. He had moved toward her and slipped under her belly. His blade slashed across her girth, but rather than cutting her open like Saundra expected the blade sang as if striking stone. The unicorn galloped past him as Max covered himself again in his dark robe.

With Max distracted by the circling unicorn, Saundra made a circle with a tiny zig-zag in the middle with her wand as she imagined her spell again. A bolt flashed from it and engulfed Max.

In her mind she wanted to see him fall to the ground, but the enveloping blast seemed to sink into the green of his cloak instead. As she was preparing another spell, her first bolt flashed out of his cloak and accelerated back at her.

She could not avoid it.

It struck her in the chest.

She felt its sting for a moment and then nothing.

Her arms flew up into the air, and her wand flew from her now numb fingers.

As she fell backward the hood of her cape fell off of her head. Max's eyes were wide as he watched her fall. She thought she felt the ground beneath her as blackness overtook her.

Chapter 7 – Yeomen Past and Present

W hen Saundra woke up she was no longer in the kingdom. She was no longer in the woods surrounding the farm. Instead, she was in a strange bed, in a place she had never been before. Her mother was sitting at the end of the strange bed with her sister. Her head still felt very woozy. The clock on the bedside table was not clear because she was not wearing her glasses, so she could not be sure how long she had been unconscious.

"Hey, kiddo," her sister said when she noticed that her eyes were open.

Saundra smiled, happy to see a friendly face but still not sure where she was and why.

"Where am I?"

"You're in the hospital, silly."

"Why?" She could not believe she needed to be in the hospital.

"Because you were unconscious when Max found

you in the woods," her mother answered in her most comforting, quiet, and dangerous tone.

"I didn't do anything wrong, mommy."

Her mother stood up and stroked her hair away from her face. "I know you didn't, sweetheart."

Saundra had no idea what had really happened. She had no idea what her mother knew. "I'm not sure what…what happened."

Kelly sat down on the foot of her bed and started telling her what they knew.

"A horse, a big mare, which had only been in the stables for a few days, was spooked by all the kids. It jumped the fence. Somehow, you were caught up in its harness."

Saundra knew there had not been a harness on the horse, but she didn't correct the story.

"It dragged you into the woods. It must have dragged you through some briars because you're a little cut up."

Saundra raised her hand to her nose and found the bandage her subconscious had been trying to tell her about.

"Yep, your nose has the deepest cut. They glued it shut with superglue." Kelly's eyes sparkled as she shared the details with her.

"They say that it's clean enough that it will probably heal without a scar, though," her mother said to console her. Saundra had never been vain about her looks and hadn't even worried about the possible scar. Her mother's attention to it, however, was a sign of how distracted she was.

"Yep," Kelly continued, "and Max, the boy you told me about. He chased after you and the horse. Somehow you broke loose. He found you lying next to a big tree. They haven't found the horse yet."

"I think that's enough, don't you, Kelly?"

Kelly looked down at her fingers at being chastised. Saundra watched her sister shut down and fade back into the bookworm she had become.

"How do you feel?" her mother asked with genuine concern.

"Hungry," Saundra answered. It was the only sensation she was feeling.

"I guess so. You didn't have lunch, and it's getting late," her mother responded. "We'll get them to bring your dinner now."

"We're eating here? Aren't we going home?"

"Not until tomorrow."

"Why?"

"They want to keep you overnight, just to make sure."

"Oh." She was not sure how she felt about staying in a hospital overnight, but she realized doctors didn't usually consider her opinion before making their decisions.

"When you've had dinner, you have visitors," Kelly said. Their mother shook her head like something was silly.

"Visitors?"

"Your teacher and some of your classmates have been waiting for you to wake up."

"Really?" She was embarrassed that anyone had been waiting for her at all. "Can I see them now?" she asked with a sudden excitement she had not expected.

"I need to talk to the doctors if I can, and get you some food. I guess it's okay."

Her mother stood up with a very relieved look on her face and left to get things organized.

Saundra smiled at the thought of visitors and then thought about exactly what Kelly had said. "Kelly, is Max out there?"

"Of course he's out there. He followed you into the woods. He helped them find you. He's a hero."

"Oh," was all she said while she was thinking how much she didn't want to see him. Her own spell—that she had cast at him—was the reason she was in the hospital being watched.

She didn't have long to worry about it, though. The door opened, and Miss Fowler walked into the room with Max and Amanda. Although the visitors were supposed to cheer her up, they actually made her feel worse. For the past few weeks she had not been spending much time with Amanda at school, and she had actually been avoiding Max. The only person that she was glad to see was Miss Fowler.

"There she is," Miss Fowler said as she stepped up to the end of her bed, much like her students walked up to her desk when she called them. "How are you feeling?"

Saundra nodded, "I'm fine. It's just a few cuts and bruises." She looked directly at Max with her comment to see his reaction, but he didn't react at all.

"I can't stay long. I just wanted to make sure you were okay."

Saundra smiled at her again.

"You know, you can sue that farm," Amanda said as plainly as if everyone else was thinking it.

Miss Fowler blushed, and Saundra could see it even in the low light of the hospital room.

Max shook his head, "That's all she talked about while we waited for you to wake up. Please tell her you don't plan to sue the farm."

"I…" She had not even thought about suing the farm. How could she explain any of what had happened? She shook her head and smiled at Amanda. "You're joking aren't you? I can't sue them anyway."

"I'm just saying," she continued. "You could sue them. You have a case. That's what my father said, anyway."

For a few minutes they talked about everything but what had happened. Then, after looking at her watch, Miss Fowler patted Amanda on the shoulder and shifted toward the door.

"Saundra, I don't expect we will see you tomorrow. I'll send your homework home to you. Come on Amanda, I need to get you home. Kelly, can you show me where your mother is? I need to talk to her."

Kelly nodded and stood up to lead Amanda and Miss Fowler out of the room. "Hey, kiddo, I'll check on your dinner while I'm out there."

Saundra wanted to scream to her sister not to leave her alone with Max, but they were gone before she could even figure out how to explain why.

Saundra crossed her arms to show him she was not interested in talking.

"I know you don't want to talk about it, but don't you think we should?"

"I'm not sure that I have anything to talk to you about. You attacked me. Look at what you did to my nose."

"They said it will heal without a scar."

"Lucky for you." She scowled at him until the soreness in her nose forced her to stop.

"I cut you in the kingdom. Why does it exist in the

real world? Don't you find that a little weird? But, even more important than that, who was the horse, and what did she want?"

"Don't you know a unicorn when you see one?"

"Yes, I do, and that was no unicorn."

"What? Of course it was."

"How did you come to that conclusion?"

"It talked to me. Horses can't talk." All she could do was parrot what the unicorn had told her because there was no other way to explain that the horse she had talked to was a unicorn.

"Really, that's it? I thought you might have more than that. Did it tell you it was a unicorn?"

"Y…" Saundra caught herself, paused for a moment to think about what she was about to say, and realized that the unicorn had never said that she really was a unicorn.

"Where was her horn?" Max asked without waiting for her to answer.

"Someone stole it."

"Stole it? Saundra, do you know what happens to a unicorn when someone cuts off its horn?"

"No," she answered without asking because his tone told her it was not good whatever it was.

"They die, Saundra. A unicorn's magic is contained in its horn. A unicorn is a magical creature. Without its magic, it can't exist."

"How do you know? You don't know that. You…" Saundra felt panic at the edge of her mind and a beeping noise from the box next to her surprised them both.

Kelly walked back in the door followed by a nurse with a tray as Saundra was about to yell something very mean at Max. Instead she swallowed it and grinned up at her sister with an unconvincing smile. The nurse walked over to the box and gave it a puzzled look. Her look moved from the box to Saundra, back to the box, and then back to Saundra.

"Whatever you two are arguing about, you should give it a rest. She needs to keep her heart rate down," the nurse chastised.

Saundra swallowed, and Max nodded.

"I'm glad you're okay," Max said. "I brought this from the farm. They left it, and I know you'll need it."

He picked up her backpack from beside him and set it on the foot of her bed. From the way it was packed she knew it held more than the few books she had packed in it for school. She assumed he had put her slippers, cape, and wand back into it. He slid it to her, and she pulled it over onto her lap. As she pulled it close, she opened the zipper and saw that she was right.

She didn't smile at him, but she looked him in the eyes with a confused look.

"Thanks, Max," she said with all of the honesty she could muster.

He nodded to everyone in the room and walked toward the door. As the nurse was pushing the tray over to her and before he walked out the door, he paused.

"Listen, Saundra. Don't believe everything someone tells you."

Before she could respond, the door closed behind him. The nurse pointed a finger at her and then the plate in front of her. Saundra grinned and turned her attention to the tray. While the nurse checked her bed, her water, and the temperature of the air, Saundra picked up the bowl of green Jello and considered what kind of spell she could cast with it. The nurse looked at her one last time and followed Max out into the hall.

Kelly, who had waited for the nurse to finish, looked at her with the unasked question on her face. She still didn't ask it as she sat down in the chair next to the bed again.

Saundra dipped her spoon into the Jello. It was the only thing on the plate that looked good. She would eat the rest later, maybe, but she needed the Jello.

"This didn't happen the way they describe it, did it?" Kelly finally finished chewing on her question and asked it.

Saundra looked over the plastic spoon in her mouth and delayed swallowing the gelatin.

"Come on, Saundra. You and Max have been back and forth on this Queen's Yeoman game. You told me about him before he showed up in school, and now he's here bringing you your backpack with the slippers and stuff you found at grandma's."

Kelly stood up from the chair and walked over to the tray.

A black and white picture was hanging between her thumb and forefinger.

There were three little girls, almost the same age as Saundra, standing on the front porch of their grandparents' house.

They were all wearing slippers of some sort.

Each one was wearing or carrying something else.

In a flash, Saundra saw three very different people on that porch.

The girl standing on the left side was wearing an intricate suit of leather armor and carried a staff and a dagger.

The one on the right was cloaked in a shimmering robe that fell to her feet and covered her head.

The third one, in the middle, was cloaked in a plate mail chest plate and carried a long sword.

She could not see their faces at all.

As soon as the image in her mind cleared, she looked up at her sister.

"Who's the one in the middle?" She knew her Aunt Ellen and her mother.

"That's Nancy Gilroy's mom."

Saundra didn't say anything.

"Those are the slippers you found." Kelly pointed to the girl on the left of the picture. "and that's the cape." She pointed to the girl on the right.

Saundra still didn't speak.

"What's going on?" Kelly asked

Saundra was not sure what to say or what her sister would really believe. Kelly knew the stories she had told her. She knew everything because she had been there to listen to it all. But, could she believe that it was touching Saundra in her real life?

Saundra started at the beginning. "The queen was killed by the dragon."

Kelly nodded and sat down on the bed next to her.

"Right, and Max came to welcome you as a Queen's Yeoman. He helped you get the slippers. You brought them home and you've told me the entire story up to when the Guardian threw you out of the tower. Is that the same tower Nancy fell out of?"

Saundra nodded.

Kelly swallowed. "This stuff is really happening to you?"

Saundra nodded.

Kelly reached out and hugged her sister. Saundra felt a sudden lightness like she had set down a backpack full of books. "How is that possible?" she whispered in her ear.

"Kelly, it really happened to Aunt Ellen, mom, and Nancy's mom. Nancy was really thrown out of the tower by the Guardian to scare her out of the kingdom because she was after something."

"What? You didn't tell me that." Kelly released her and stood up as she responded.

"I know, I didn't tell you that Max was working with the Guardian either."

Kelly shook her head. "Okay, so what was she looking for that was so important that they would try to kill her?"

"I think she was looking for the unicorn's horn."

"Unicorn, what unicorn?"

Saundra smiled when she realized she had not actually told her sister about the unicorn.

"The horse at the farm recognized me because I was wearing the slippers. It told me about a girl that had come into the kingdom and had taken its horn."

"It was the unicorn?"

"I think so. I'm not sure, though."

"Why not?"

"Because, Max said a unicorn can't survive if someone cuts off its horn."

"He's right," Kelly said without really giving it any thought.

"How do you know?"

"I read. A lot."

Saundra could not argue with that.

"The unicorn wanted me to find its horn. It wanted me to help it fix the kingdom, and it can if I can find its horn."

Kelly frowned at that.

"What?"

"I don't know. I guess I've read too many stories. It sounds like a trick."

"But, unicorns can't lie."

Kelly thought about her logic and shook her head. "I guess."

"So you agree with Max?" Saundra asked, unable to keep the frown off of her face.

"I'm not sure."

"I need more information. Kelly, I want to try something."

"What?"

"I can't tell you, I just have to try it."

"I'm not going to like this, am I?"

"I don't know. Are you going home tonight?"

"Yeah, Dad's coming to take me home so I can go to school tomorrow."

"Okay, you'll see later."

Kelly looked at her sister like she could be losing her mind. Saundra just smiled.

After that they let the conversation turn to more childish stuff until Saundra completed her dinner. Her mother returned, and they both visited with her even though Saundra wanted to ask her about the picture. She didn't have a bowl of soup, so she left it alone.

When her father came for Kelly, she got the rare pleasure of getting to talk to him before she went to sleep. He couldn't stay long; he had to take Kelly home before it was too late.

Because she was in the hospital for observation, she had several visitors throughout the night, but they didn't give her any medication that made her sleepy.

She fought her own desire to sleep until her mother was asleep on the couch, and it was time for her sister to be in bed.

In the dark of her hospital room, Saundra tried for the first time to enter the kingdom and intentionally bring someone else with her.

Max said she had done it to him before. That was how she was able to sneak into his imagination while he was visiting the Guardian, but Saundra was not really sure that it worked. She wasn't even sure how to really make it happen.

She focused on imagining a room in the queen's castle where they could meet. When the room appeared around her, there was a long wooden table with a silken runner and four candelabras. Each one was filled with burning candles that lit the room. Once she knew the room was right, she focused on who she wanted with her.

A heavy wooden door strapped together with hammered iron bands and large studs opened, and her sister stepped into the room. She was dressed in a green cotehardi with sleeves that tapered open from her elbows to the floor. Her hair was pulled back in a braid contained by a sheer crispinette with a circlet of matching cloth and silver. In her left hand she was carrying a large tome and a quill. Saundra almost didn't recognize her, but Kelly knew immediately where she was.

"How have you done this? I'm asleep. Why are you in my dream? Where am I?"

"You're in the kingdom, and I've brought you here so we can get to the bottom of this."

"How are we going to do that?"

"We aren't, not until my other guest joins us."

Kelly set her heavy tome down on the table and looked at Saundra like she had three eyes. The stare didn't last long before the door opened again and a third girl entered the room. She was wearing a full suit of plate armor. The polished surface reflected the candle light back into Saundra's eyes. The young woman's head was uncovered, and she carried her helm under her left arm. She looked around the room. Her face reddened, and her eyes squinted as she recognized where she was. Without stepping farther into the room she pointed her gauntleted hand at Saundra.

"Why am I here? I can never come back here. I nearly died here. I will not be drug back into this again."

She turned to walk out the door. Saundra called after her. "Nancy, wait."

At the calling of her name, Nancy stopped and looked back at Saundra.

"I need your help."

"I don't care. I cannot go through this again."

"We need your help, Nancy. The kingdom needs your help," Kelly said while looking at Saundra to make sure what she was saying was true.

Nancy spun around in the armored suit faster than Saundra believed possible. Her sword was out of its sheath and pointing at Saundra instead of her finger. Kelly took two steps back at the action, surprised by its violence. Saundra realized that she had not really been in the kingdom without their grandmother. Her sister was not prepared for any of this.

"I'll not be fooled again," Nancy shouted. "I'll not be threatened by the Queen's Yeomen either. I'll kill you where you sit and never think about it again. That beast will not chase me in my dreams anymore. I'll not be played with. You let me leave this nightmare, or I promise I'll kill you."

"I'm not here to threaten you. We're not here to fight you. The guardian is not here. All I want to know is why he tried to kill you."

"How do I know? How can I ever trust anyone? The guardian said I was committing treason against the queen. He said I was going to destroy the kingdom when all I ever wanted was to protect it. I was going to make it safe forever," she cried. "I can't tell you. I can never tell anyone."

"You were looking for the unicorn's horn," Saundra said.

The tip of Nancy's sword dipped a little.

"How do you know about that?"

"The unicorn came to me, too. It told me about the horn. It said it can save the kingdom with it."

"Nancy, this is serious. We need your help," Kelly said.

"You don't think I know this is serious? I nearly died when the Guardian threw me out of that tower."

"Why did he throw you out? Does he have the horn?" Saundra swallowed hard at the thought of returning to that tower and confronting the Guardian. She might have to if she wanted the horn.

"No," Nancy answered and dropped her sword to her side. "He has the key."

No one said anything for a moment. Saundra let that news settle.

"If you know about the key, you must know where the horn is. You must know how to get it." Kelly broke the silence and tried to help Saundra get an answer. Saundra could see in Nancy's eyes how much she wanted to complete her mission. She could see how much she wanted to find the horn.

"The horn's not in the kingdom. That's why no one can find it," Nancy answered. "I found that out from my mother. She said that they had taken it out of the kingdom to keep it safe."

"They who?" Saundra asked.

"My mother, your mother, and your aunt. They found it in the kingdom, but it was too dangerous to leave there. We inherited the job of protecting it, and I failed on my first mission. I was too weak to face the Guardian."

"Where did they hide it?"

"She didn't know. Once they had it outside, your mother and aunt hid it. They gave my mother the key. She gave it to the Guardian. That was how I knew to look for the key first. Once I had it I was going to search for the horn. Either your mother or your aunt knows where the horn is."

Saundra looked at Kelly, who shook her head. Neither of them had ever seen a horn. They had no idea where it might be.

"Nancy, I'm sorry this has been difficult for you. I may need your help when it's time to recover the horn. Together we might be able to face the Guardian," Saundra said.

"No," Nancy said and shook her head. "Let me out of here. I can't be in here. Not ever again." She turned away from the sisters and walked back toward the door.

"Nancy! Don't make me force you to help when it's time."

Nancy scowled over her shoulder. "Remember my warning. Force me and you will have two enemies."

"Don't you want to complete your mission?" Kelly asked quietly. Nancy's angry façade collapsed.

"You know I do."

"We can do this together."

Saundra nodded at what her sister offered and looked at Nancy.

"It's our responsibility now."

Without saying yes or no, she walked out the door and closed it behind her.

Saundra shook her head. "She's terrified of the kingdom, but she was close to solving this puzzle. She almost had the key, and I know where it is."

"Did you see it when you were in the tower before?"

"No, but I saw where he reached when he thought about it. I know where the key is."

"Then we need to go get it."

Saundra started to say no.

"You can't face him alone. He'll do the same thing to you that he did to Nancy."

"He already tried. I'm not going to be afraid of him. But, if we can face him without Max interfering, we might be able to get the key from him."

"And then what?"

"When we have the key, we show it to mom. Maybe she'll tell us where the horn is."

"Why did they take it out of the kingdom? Why do they even have it?"

"I think Aunt Ellen took it from the unicorn."

"Saundra, you can't believe that Ellen killed a unicorn."

"I don't. I think she took its horn."

"But that would kill it."

"Then how did it talk to me this afternoon?"

Kelly didn't answer her.

Saundra felt sure her plan would work, if she could get the key from the Guardian. That was not going to be easy since that was his primary job. She would need to think about that. She said her goodbyes to her sister and ended the session in the kingdom before she fell asleep. As soon as she was released from the hospital, Saundra would need a plan to face the Guardian and take his key. This time, she was not going to face him alone.

Chapter 8 – Taking the Key

S aundra returned to school on the Friday following their field trip with her plan for getting the key prepared and rehearsed. She had planned it all while the doctors and nurses completed their observations. She had considered everything her sister and Nancy had told her. She took into account Max's side of the argument. She couldn't solve everything, but she needed the key to find the horn.

Her biggest concern was Max. He was not going to give up. For her plan to work, she had to convince him that he had nothing to worry about. Thinking about it as she walked toward the door to her classroom, it seemed impossible, but it was too late to change her plan now. For the first time in weeks she sought Max out as soon as she arrived at school.

"Morning, Max," she said over her shoulder as she walked past him at the homework slots. He looked back immediately, as she had expected, because her greeting was out of character.

She refused to watch him as she took her seat and prepared for class. It was nearly as difficult to pay attention that day as it had been when Max had convinced her to hold out her homework, but this time she was not terrified. She was not going to pass out from anxiety and throw up all over the teacher. She had prepared for what was to come.

All through the morning, Max kept looking over at her, and she continued to act as if nothing in the world was wrong. By the time the bell rang for lunch, she knew Max would come to find her. That was when the hard work would start.

She walked slowly to the cafeteria, alone. She bought a lunch and sat down at a table, alone.

Not long after she had selected her table and settled her lunch around her, Max appeared with his own lunch and a curious look on his face.

"What are you up to?" he asked and set his tray down across from her.

"I'm having lunch—apparently with you."

"You never have lunch like this."

"Max, I was thrown out of a tower on the playground and nearly run down by a horse. Remember?"

"Yeah. So?"

"So, I'm traumatized by my encounter. Some change in behavior has to be expected, or at least that's what the doctors told my mother."

Saundra dipped her spoon into her tomato soup, circled the bowl once, lifted it above the steam, stuck it into her mouth, and savored the tangy flavor. Maybe it wasn't magic, but it was tasty.

"Okay, I'm in. What's going on?"

"I'm done. I'm not going back to the kingdom."

Max paused and looked at her. His eyes projected his disbelief. She had expected no less.

"There's no way. You can't stay away."

"Why not? Nancy doesn't visit anymore. It's too dangerous. The guardian and this encounter with the horse have convinced me of that. I'm not going back. I'm too scared."

Max nearly laughed at her. "Saundra, the kingdom is part of you. After we first met, I thought the Guardian might be able to scare you away, but you bring it with you everywhere you go. You draw people into it with you from wherever they are. You're always connected to it."

"No, I'm pretty sure I can stay away if I want to," she said flatly and savored another bite of her soup. "You should tell the Guardian that I'm no longer a threat to him. He's done his job. Whatever he's guarding is safe."

Max considered her statement. She couldn't tell if he believed her or not. It was possible he knew she didn't really believe what she was saying.

"You should tell him yourself." His answer was proof he didn't.

"Why?"

"He needs to know about your encounter with the unicorn."

"Don't you mean horse?" She paused. "Why should I tell him about the unicorn if I'm not going back? I'm the only person the unicorn has approached. It's over."

"You need to tell him about the meeting. He needs to know that something is after the horn."

"Why? If I'm not going after it, it's safe."

"No. It's not."

"Why not, Max?" He was not giving up on her meeting with the Guardian again. She was not going to agree, but she really wanted to know why it was so important that he know about it. "The unicorn can't get to the horn alone, or it already would have. I'm not going to look for it. It's over."

"It's never over."

Saundra dipped her spoon into her soup and looked at him. "What do you mean? What aren't you telling me?"

Max looked at her like he was caught in a trap.

She extracted her spoon from the bowl and pointed it at him. "Tell me what this is all about."

"Your unicorn is the dragon."

"What makes you say that? You don't know that."

"I know the legends."

"So, tell me how the legends say I was talking to a dragon the other day."

"It pulled you and me both into the kingdom from here. It found you and identified you by your slippers."

He wasn't even trying. Saundra was getting agitated. "So, a unicorn could have done that. According to you, I could have done that."

"Saundra, the unicorn is dead."

"So this is another unicorn."

Max shook his head in frustration. "There isn't another unicorn. The only unicorn died when its horn was cut off."

Saundra had not considered that there was only one unicorn. She hadn't asked her sister about that.

To avoid her confusion and to keep from admitting he had a point, she asked another question she had on her mind. "Who cut off the unicorn's horn?"

"I don't know."

"I thought you did. You acted like you did." She stirred the soup in her bowl a little.

"No. How could I? It happened so long ago."

Again, his answer surprised her. She started to wonder if she had really listened to her grandmother tell the stories at all. She was convinced he was going to say that her aunt had cut off the horn.

"Who did you think cut off the unicorn's horn?"

"I don't know," she lied.

"Saundra, the unicorn and the dragon had fought over the kingdom since the beginning. Long ago, a little girl who had been tricked by the dragon cut off the horn of the unicorn. It nearly destroyed the kingdom. If she had delivered the horn to the dragon, it would have."

Saundra stopped him. "What little girl?"

"I don't know." His frustration was clear in his voice. "No one does. It's such an old legend that the name and her story have become lost in the history. She was very young. The dragon deceived her. No one knows how." Max fended off her next question and continued. "She's the reason the Queen's Yeomen exist."

"It goes back that far?"

"That's what I'm telling you. No one knows who took the unicorn's horn, but we know who it was taken for. She was supposed to take it to the dragon. At the last moment, she realized the dragon had deceived her, and she hid the horn somewhere in the kingdom. She was the first Queen's Yeoman."

"So what does this have to do with my aunt?"

"Your aunt was a Queen's Yeoman. Every generation, the dragon approaches a young girl in the Queen's Yeomen and asks her to bring it the horn. It always finds a way to convince her that the only way to save the kingdom is to find the horn. The dragon never appears as itself. What little girl is going to help a dragon take over the kingdom? I think, based on what happened to you, that it's pretending to be the unicorn."

"You're saying my aunt was the one that the dragon approached before."

"I don't know what happened with your aunt. I'm just guessing."

"Then why did you say she was an agent of the dragon?"

"Because I thought she was. The guardian was protecting the horn in his keep until she took it. The guardian knows how important the horn is. It's the biggest threat to the kingdom. That's why he was guarding it."

"How do you know all of this?"

"Saundra, my grandfather is the Guardian. He tells me the old stories of the kingdom when I visit him at the nursing home."

Saundra, shocked by his revelation, sat back in her seat. Her plan was to take the key from the Guardian. She stared at her bowl for a moment and thought about what he said. She was not sure she could take the key from Max's grandfather.

How did he know the old stories? Her grandmother had told her the stories for years until she died. How could he be the Guardian? Her grandmother had been the source of the stories, but now Max was telling her there was another source.

Thinking about her grandmother made her think about the funeral and indirectly about the dragon who had killed her. A cold stone settled into her stomach as she thought about it and she had a sudden fear for Max's grandfather. He was the only remaining guardian, not only of the key but of the kingdom.

"Max, the dragon killed my grandmother. She was the queen."

Max stared at her.

"How does your grandfather know the old stories of the kingdom?"

"I don't know. He makes them up and tells them to me when I visit him. I didn't think the queen was a real person."

"Did you ever meet my grandmother? Maybe she told you the stories?"

"No, I've not met her. My grandfather told me the stories."

"But you were in my grandparents' house. You knew about my mirror. You knew about the slippers."

"No, I don't know how I knew about that. You pulled me in that time. I was asleep. I don't know how I knew those things."

The more she thought about it, the more Saundra felt sure that Max's grandfather was at risk.

"Max, if the dragon kills your grandfather…"

Max didn't let her finish what she was thinking. He shook his head. "No, he's fine. The dragon can't kill the Guardian."

"The dragon killed the queen, Max. If the dragon kills the Guardian, the dragon will take the key."

"No!" he shouted.

Saundra didn't say anything more.

Max stood up from the table and walked away. He

didn't look back. His chin was on his chest as he crossed the cafeteria.

Saundra finished her soup, sure, now more than before, that she was making the right choice to go after the key. There was no way she could convince Max that his grandfather was at risk from the dragon. Her plan to keep Max away had failed, but she had no choice now. She had to secure the kingdom. If the unicorn was the dragon, and she was not sure she believed that it was, she would have to think much harder about giving it the horn. But first she needed the key. With it she would find the horn.

The rest of that day Max stayed away from her. She didn't see him on the playground, but she had not looked for him either. Twice, in class, she had caught him looking at her with a look that could have been sadness but she took as anger. By the end of the day she was convinced there was no way they would ever be friends, that the dragon would go after the Guardian, and that if she didn't take the key first the horn would be at risk.

When she got home, she sat down and told Kelly about their conversation. She verified everything he had said. She believed that the dragon was probably trying to get the horn and kill the Guardian, even though she didn't really believe that the dragon had killed their grandmother. When she asked Saundra what she was planning, she shared most of her idea. Kelly approved of most of it even though it meant she was going to have to be involved. When they were done, Saundra gave her their mother's cape and they both went to bed.

After they had eaten breakfast Saundra grabbed her backpack, motioned for her sister to follow her, and ran across their yard to one of her favorite places among the trees. On weekends and particularly hard days she would hide among the limbs and daydream.

When they were out of sight of the house, she pulled on the slippers and took out her wand.

"Are you ready?" she asked.

"Oh, you're asking now?"

Saundra shook her head. "We are a team," she answered and then immediately imagined where she wanted to be.

In a moment they were in a gray room that was not stone or any kind of material she had seen before. In the middle of the room, there was a metal card table with stools surrounding it. Kelly sat down at the table with Saundra.

"Now, we need one more team member," Saundra said as she focused on finding Nancy. It didn't take long before the armored knight she had met at the hospital appeared in the room.

"I figured you would be looking for me soon. Where are we? This isn't the kingdom."

"You're right," Saundra said. "But that is." She pointed into the darkened corner of her imaginary room at a wooden door strapped with metal bands.

"If this isn't the kingdom, then where are we?" Kelly asked as she looked around the room.

"I told Max I was not going back to the kingdom anymore. I lied a little because I needed him to be a little more relaxed. When that failed I decided he would tell his grandfather, the Guardian, and they would be ready for us to come through the kingdom. This is a space I created where we can enter and leave the kingdom and not be observed or followed."

Nancy nodded at the idea.

Kelly looked impressed.

"When we open that door, we will be entering the Guardian's keep on the top floor. We have to take the key from him."

Nancy shuddered a little, and Saundra watched her hand grip the pommel of her sword.

"When everyone is ready, I'll open the door. We'll take him by surprise."

Nancy nodded at her, but Saundra could still see doubt in her eyes.

"Nancy, I'm not going to let him hurt you."

"Then let's get this over with."

Kelly nodded that she was ready, and they all three walked over to the door. Saundra looked back at them and reached for the knob. Nancy drew her sword and lifted the blade into a two-handed brace.

Kelly was not carrying her book, but she was wearing their mother's cape. She pulled the hood over her head and disappeared.

Saundra reached for the knob and readied her wand.

The opening on the kingdom side was not a doorway. Part of the outside wall of the keep slid open like a door on the top floor where the Guardian was standing. He was looking out over the plateau around his keep. Max was standing beside him.

Saundra walked through the opening with her wand out and pointed at the Guardian. She had forgotten to cast her planned protective spell over them before opening the door. It was too late to turn back; so, she changed spells quickly, cast the protection over them, and then quickly refocused her wand on the Guardian.

When they were all through the opening, she

walked across the floor toward him. Nancy, who had seemed nervous and afraid on the other side, charged across the floor with her sword raised to strike. Her action was such a surprise that none of the suits of armor reacted until she was already past them.

Max was the only person to see her attack, and his response came at the last moment. His sword flashed up in time to deflect her blow to her left. He stepped between her and the Guardian.

Saundra could not focus on Nancy for long because a suit of the animated armor was coming after her. She zapped it with a quick spell that turned it to stone. It stopped in place, but others were coming for her.

Kelly, who not even Saundra could see, seemed to be able to move without attracting attention. Saundra guessed this because all of the armor was moving toward her and Nancy.

One of the two guards nearest to the Guardian struck Nancy across the back as Max was keeping her focus away from her target. The loud crash of metal on metal rang out across the plateau like a gong, and Nancy dropped to her knees from the strike's power. Recovering quickly, she spun around on her knees driving her sword ahead of her as she turned to cleave the suit of armor in half. She continued her spin onto one knee and stood up to face Max again.

"Stop!" The order came from the Guardian. His own animated guards stopped and looked at him. Saundra held her next spell. Nancy and Max maintained a face to face stance with swords touching.

Kelly was standing next to the Guardian with her hood down. Saundra thought that he might have captured her at first; but his rod was at his side, and she was not attacking him.

"Max, put your sword away."

Max looked at his grandfather for a moment, shocked that he would give in like this.

"Nancy, I'm sorry I hurt you. Put down your sword. Nothing here will hurt you again."

"What's going on, Kelly?" Saundra asked her sister. This was not the way she had planned this to go.

"I thought about your plan last night. I thought about everything you told me and I thought I might, if I had a chance, just talk to the Guardian. After listening to our grandmother tell the stories I just felt that anyone who knew them as well as you said he did had to know her. I took a chance," Kelly answered.

"And she was right to do it," the Guardian said. "Until I met Saundra, I had no idea that any of you were real. I've been creating stories in the kingdom since I was your age. The first ones I created with a young girl I knew at school. We built such a beautiful world together that I kept telling stories even after my parents moved to another town. Sometimes I believed that she was still meeting me here to build the stories, but I never thought it was really possible for our worlds to go on touching after we were separated."

Saundra was not sure what the Guardian was saying. She looked at Kelly with a puzzled look on her face. Kelly was smiling a broad smile.

"Kelly, what's this all about?"

"This kingdom came from stories our grandmother shared with her daughters and then with us. She also shared them with Nancy's mother, which is how Nancy came to be here."

"And, I know of the kingdom because of my grandfather," Max added. Kelly nodded.

"Right. You see, our grandmother created the stories she shared with another person, Max's grandfather."

Saundra was starting to understand it.

"I'm sad to hear of her passing, and I wish I had known. I would have attended the funeral."

Saundra looked at the Guardian and saw genuine sadness in his eyes. She found the man she had first disliked to be quite a friendly person. Sadness hit her when she realized she still had to take the key.

"I'm still not sure how this is able to happen," the Guardian said.

"The kingdom is an important place to us. When the queen died, it suffered. I don't want to see it destroyed," Saundra said. "The dragon killed the queen, and I think it is after you."

The guardian looked at her with gentle eyes that she had not been able to see before. He looked at her like she knew something no one else did.

"I'm afraid you're right."

Max's jaw dropped, and he looked at his grandfather. He couldn't speak.

"The dragon comes for us all," he said calmly to his grandson. "You'll be fine without me. This young woman you've met can help you deal with it in the same way she has dealt with her grandmother's death. I'm sorry I hadn't told you, Max."

Max looked at Saundra, and she thought she could see a sign of embarrassment. She smiled at him to keep him from feeling bad. Then she looked up at the Guardian again.

"I don't want the kingdom to be destroyed. I don't want to lose it. You have something that can't fall into the hands of the dragon. Will you please give me the key? I need it to protect the kingdom."

The guardian dropped down onto one knee and reached into his blouse. When he pulled it out, he was holding the end of a gold chain and a small skeleton key. He removed the key from the chain and handed it to her.

"I've been the Guardian for a long time. I will miss protecting this place for you, but I have no doubt I'm passing it into the right hands."

When she took the key from him, he wrapped his big hands around hers and pulled Max's hand over to hers.

"Work together to take care of the kingdom," the Guardian said when their hands touched.

She and Max both dropped to one knee in front of the Guardian as he bestowed their duty on them. He motioned for Nancy and Kelly to come over as well.

When they both reached him and knelt before him he reached into a pouch hanging from his sash and pulled out two rings. He placed one ring on Saundra's hand and another one on Nancy's.

Saundra looked at him, disappointed that he had not given one to Kelly. Then he raised a finger to indicate he was not done.

"Rise, yeomen. You are now charged with protecting the kingdom. But, you Kelly, you have a duty beyond what the yeomen are here for. You're here to build the kingdom."

From a shelf on the wall behind him he pulled the book Kelly had carried the last time Saundra had pulled her in. Kelly took the book and nodded at the charge the Guardian had left her.

The Guardian nodded and stood up. He looked out at his kingdom and smiled. When he pulled Max over to him to look out over the walls again, Saundra motioned for Kelly and Nancy to follow her. They exited back through the hidden door they had come through.

The next day, Max called Saundra to tell her that his grandfather had passed away in his sleep. The guardian was gone. Saundra cried with him. She had the key. She knew who could tell her where the horn was. When Saundra and Max returned to the kingdom to lock up the Guardian's tower, the dark clouds that seemed to surround everything told them something was very wrong. Maybe, if she could find the horn, they could save the kingdom. Maybe they would not be too late. Saundra tried to convince herself, but in her heart she was beginning to wonder if the kingdom could really survive with no queen and no guardian.

Chapter 9 – The Key and The Horn

W hen Saundra hung up the phone, it was obvious to everyone else that she had bad news. Her mother looked at her with a very worried frown, and Kelly simply shook her head as if she already knew.

"What's wrong, Saundra?" her mother asked.

Saundra looked over at her mother and thought about what she wanted to say. She was convinced her mother knew where the horn was, but she was not sure how to ask the question. How did you ask someone where they were hiding a powerful magic item?

After giving it more thought than usual, she surrendered to her own nature and walked across the room. Without a word she took the key from her pocket and sat it on the table in front of her mother.

Her mother did nothing to hide the recognition that crossed her face. She didn't even seem surprised.

"Where did you find that?" she asked with a lilt of amazement in her voice.

"So you recognize this key?"

Her mother squeezed her eyebrows together and tilted her head at Saundra.

"Of course, but I never thought I would see it again. We lost that key before you were born."

Saundra stepped back a bit. She had been ready to interrogate her mother, but she seemed to have no idea of the power of that key. Still unconvinced, Saundra looked her mother directly in the eyes.

"The dragon killed the Guardian."

Again her mother's reaction was less than Saundra expected. Was it possible she was wrong? Was it possible that Aunt Ellen was the only one who knew what the key opened?

"Saundra, stop being so dramatic. What are you talking about? Who is the Guardian?"

"Mother," Kelly said as she left the wall where she had been watching the exchange. "Don't you remember the stories grandma told you when you were young? The same stories she told me and Suandra. Don't you remember being a Queen's Yeoman?"

Their mother looked up at Kelly as if she had voiced some magic spell. She sat back in the chair and held the key up in front of her as if studying it might make it go away.

"I don't want to talk about that." She carefully laid the key on the table and stood up to leave the room.

"But, mommy…"

"Saundra, Aunt Ellen is right. You need to grow up," her mother snapped as she walked out of the kitchen.

Saundra felt crushed by her mother's words. She wobbled a little and sat down on the edge of the chair.

"Saundra you can't give up now," Kelly cried. "You have to keep trying."

It took a moment for Saundra to shake off the feeling that she had just been slapped in the face. When she finally did, she still was not sure what to do next. Her mother knew what the key meant. She knew how important it was. She had been a Queen's Yeoman.

Unsure of what to do, she collected the key and rushed upstairs to her room. As she walked through the doorway, a voice from her dresser surprised her.

"Saundra, you must do something now. The kingdom is at risk. You can't wait any longer," the mirror cried.

Saundra stared at it. It had never spoken to her without her first asking it a question. For it to speak first meant there had to be real trouble.

"What's happening?"

"The dragon is closing portals into the kingdom. If it closes them all, there will be no way to enter the kingdom. It will die away."

"What can I do? I don't have the horn."

"Get it," the rectangle of glass whined from the top of her dresser.

Saundra closed her door and walked down the hall to her mother's room. She barged through the door without knocking and was shocked by what she saw. Her mother was lying on her bed and sobbing.

"Mommy, what's wrong?"

She looked up from the edge of the bed. Her eyes were red and puffy.

"You spend so much time in that world. You can't live there, Saundra," her mother moaned. "We did, for way too long. But, we had to grow up, and so will you. My mother, created that world. She's dead, and I just don't want to think about it."

"Do you want it to die, too? Do you want the world she created to cease to exist? If you don't help me, it's going to."

"Saundra, please go away." Her mother buried her head in the covers again and sobbed.

Saundra surrendered for the moment and walked out of the room. She needed to convince her mother that she had to help. How could she make her want to save the kingdom?

As she entered her bedroom again, she looked at the mirror and had a thought.

"You're a portal to the kingdom, aren't you?"

"One of the last remaining."

"Take me to it."

"You have but to ask."

In an instant, Saundra was standing on the plateau looking toward both the tower and the castle. They both represented the strongholds of the previous creators, and they were both in flames. An enormous winged beast stroked at the wind and smoke as it circled the devastation. Its black scales shimmered in the sunlight as it reveled in the destruction. A suit of armor stoically armed the catapult and fired a globe of something at the dragon.

Saundra watched as the green glass sphere flew through the air and impacted the side of the dragon. It broke and engulfed the beast in a cloud of gas. It took several thrusts upward for it to break away from the cloud. Once it was free, it was clear that the brown-green cloud had hurt it, but it was not enough. Before the lone suit of armor could load the catapult again, the dragon was above the tower blasting a stream of fire down onto the top floor. The suit jiggled about as if it was on a hot stove and danced in the stream of fire as Saundra watched its metal body melt into the stone floor. The rope on the catapult burned away, and the wood glowed red as the fire consumed it.

Saundra could not believe the massive power of the magical beast, and she wondered if there was any power that could stand against it. She was not ready to try, so she hid among the trees until it had flown back to assault the walls of the castle again.

"Mirror, I'm going to need your help with this one. I've never tried to break through to an adult."

She had no idea if it even heard her, but she focused on her plan anyway. First she thought of her mother as she had seen her in the picture. With that image in her mind she searched through the imaginations she could interact with until she found the little girl. As soon as she knew where she was, she latched onto her consciousness and pulled her into the kingdom.

A girl, dressed like she had been in the picture, stood before Saundra. She was confused and angry. Saundra stared at her. Each stared at the other, struggling with what had happened. Saundra could not understand why she looked like the young girl in the picture and not her full-grown mother.

"Saundra, what have you done?" the girl asked.

"What I had to," Saundra answered, shaking off the temporary stupor.

"You've pulled me into the kingdom, again. How

dare you!"

"I had to show you. I had to take a chance that you cared enough about it to save it. I had to take a chance that you would do it again."

"Saundra, I can't save it."

"Why not? I don't want to lose it." Saundra felt the warm tear run down her cheek as she felt the hopelessness seep into her bones. "None of us want to lose the kingdom. Even Kelly wants to save it, and she's barely even been here. You have to help me. All I need is the horn, and then I can save it."

"No, you can't. The queen, who created it, is dead. The guardian, who protected it, is dead now, too. Saundra, there's nothing you can do."

"I have to try. I can't give up." Saundra raised her hand and showed her the ring the Guardian had given her. "I'm a Queen's Yeoman, and I will not surrender."

Saundra had lost sight of the dragon as she had argued with her mother. While they had been talking, it had slipped across the plateau to investigate the movement in the trees. As her mother was shaking her head in response to her dogged commitment, it was plummeting toward them.

Her mother jumped at her to grab her. Saundra was not sure what to do. She brought her hands up to guard against the attack from her mother. The hand Saundra thought was going to hit her, grabbed her shoulder.

"Run! It's spotted us," her mother shouted as she tried to move Saundra from her spot.

Saundra stared up at the huge black and gray bulk that was descending from the sky at them. Its angry eyes and age-yellowed teeth frightened her more than anything ever had. She couldn't move even though it was nearly upon them.

"Saundra, come on!" her mother screamed and tugged at her.

It was too late to run. It was too late to hide. There was nothing that would save them from the dragon as it plunged toward her.

She shivered as she thought about what was about to happen.

"Saundra, if you're not going to run, you have to save us. You got us both in here. Now, get us out!" her mother shouted.

The dragon's jaws opened and the first tendrils of fire appeared at the back of its throat. Her mother's words reminded her that there was an escape. As she fought with her mind to create the path out, Saundra felt the fingers of panic release her. She pointed at the ground and released her plan into the magical realm. They both fell into the darkness of the ground that opened up beneath them.

Fire engulfed the space where they had just been standing, and Saundra wondered if her escape was too late. The fire was pursuing them as if the dragon was trying to reach across the barrier. Saundra could feel the heat and the fear from before gripping her just as the heavy wood and metal door closed, cutting off the pursuing fire. Together they rolled across the floor that was suddenly beneath them as their fall became a slide.

"Where are we now?" her mother asked.

"Nowhere," Saundra answered with a puff of relief.

"We can't be nowhere, Saundra. Nowhere doesn't exist."

"Well, I don't know where this is. It's not the kingdom, and it's not anywhere else. I think of it as my personal closet to the kingdom."

"You created this."

"When I needed a way to get into the kingdom that was secret, I created it."

"Why is it so plain? That's not like your imagination."

"I'm not sure. It just is."

"Hmm. Can we get out of here?"

"You just have to want to leave."

In a flash, her mother vanished. A little hurt that she didn't want to stay any longer, Saundra looked around at the room with its simple table and its heavy door to the kingdom.

"I kinda like it. It's peaceful," she said to no one before leaving the room behind.

Back in her bedroom she sat up on her bed to find her mother standing in the doorway with the key between her fingers. Saundra grinned up at her hopefully.

"You can't save the kingdom with the horn."

"Why not?"

"Saundra, it's not yours. We've all been living in that kingdom for a long time. The creators are gone. All we could ever do as yeomen was protect it. There is no way to keep it from destroying itself now that its authors are gone. Maybe, it's time for you to move on."

"No, I can't. I need the kingdom."

"Do you? Aren't you capable of creating your own place? Didn't you already?"

Saundra shook her head and looked down at the floor.

"You created a place that added on to another person's world. You expanded something we have only lived in."

"It's only a room."

"Sure. And the kingdom started somewhere."

"How do you know that?"

"Because I believed in it."

Saundra smiled up at her mother's sudden faith.

"Because I believe in you. You can build your own kingdom and share it with others."

"How do I do that?"

"You do what your aunt and I never learned how to do."

"What?"

"I'll show you. Get your sister and follow me."

Saundra jumped from the bed and followed her mother out of the room. As soon as she was in the hall she screamed for her sister rather than leaving her mother's side.

"Kelly! Get up here!"

Faster than Saundra had ever seen her move, Kelly was in the hallway with them and walking into their mother's room. As a trio they walked to the chest-of-drawers beside the bed and approached the old clock that their mother had taken from their grandmother's house.

Their mother turned the clock sideways and stuck the key into a small keyhole on its side. Saundra was not sure that she had ever seen the hole before, but, then again, she had never looked for it.

The lock clicked. A door opened in the side of the clock. As her mother pulled the door open, Saundra took in a breath and held it. When the magical blast failed to form—when even a quiet whoosh of air failed to escape the hidden portal—she exhaled.

She could not see what was in the clock, and she could tell her sister couldn't see anything either based on the way she was moving from side to side to look up into the clock. Their mother reached into the space behind the face where the gears of the mantle clock still spun and pulled out a long satin-covered necklace box. The black fabric skin of the box shimmered in the light of the room.

Their mother held the box in her hands for a moment. Saundra thought she saw a tear run down her cheek, and she pulled the box up and against her chest. Saundra looked at Kelly. Kelly looked back with excitement and understanding filling her eyes. They both waited quietly until their mother finished saying goodbye to her memories.

"Listen, forget what I said downstairs," she said and handed the box to Saundra. "Keep dreaming. Build your own world. Save this kingdom by making it a part of the kingdom you build. We failed to build onto it. We failed as yeomen, but you don't have to make the same mistake."

Saundra opened the box. Lying on its satin lining was the golden spiral of a unicorn's horn. She ran a finger across its glistening surface, and a shiver ran up her spine. It was still warm. Kelly reached across her to touch it, and the horn vibrated in the box as if it recognized her.

Kelly and Saundra looked at one another as the horn reacted to them. Saundra looked over at their mother.

"How do we build the world you're describing?" Saundra asked.

"I think," their mother answered as she stepped up

and put her hand on Kelly's head, "Kelly can help with that."

"Yeah," Kelly answered and nodded, "I think I can, too."

Chapter 10 – The Seed of the New Kingdom

W ith the horn and the key in hand, their mother looked up at Saundra.

"Well, do your thing. Get us to your room," she said.

Caught up in the excitement of it all, Kelly nodded next to her.

"Just a sec," she said and ran back to her room.

She grabbed the mirror from her dresser and raced back to join them around the bed.

"Can you take us all to my room instead of the kingdom?" she asked the mirror in her hand.

Kelly stared at her, perplexed, as she talked into her hand.

Her mother laughed as if she were hearing something absurd and having to accept it.

"Of course I can," it answered.

Kelly and Saundra would argue for years about when the mirror responded since it happened as they transitioned from the bedroom to the plain room with the table and the wooden door. None of them ever denied hearing the mirror answer. Either way, it did exactly what she asked.

Saundra appeared in her red cape with her green boots. Her wand was safely in her belt. Similarly her mother appeared as she had looked in the picture, wearing a cape but with no wand apparent. Her sister appeared in her elegant dress along with the book and quill. Kelly started looking around. Without delay, she set the book on the table and opened it to the last page with writing on it.

The white quill that was in her hand wiggled as she wrote feverishly into the pages. As she did, the light in the room changed. Windows and another door appeared that opened onto a brightly lit outside world.

"Hey," Saundra said, a little agitated. "I liked this place a little plain."

"I guess you'll just have to make another room of your own," Kelly answered as she threw open the door and stepped out onto a flat plain surrounded by tall mountains that looked a lot like the plateau in the old kingdom, only a lot larger. The book remained on the table, but she continued to write into the air.

In the back of Saundra's head, she buried the plan to remake her quiet and plain room and followed her sister out into the green grass. Just before she stepped out of the doorway, she looked back at the room. The old standup mirror that had been in their grandmother's house appeared in the middle of the floor next to the table. If she couldn't keep it plain, she would at least have what she wanted in it.

She ran to catch up with Kelly and their mother.

They had found a place on the plain, next to a stream that ran amongst the trees, where they stood waiting for her.

When she reached where they were waiting, her mother knelt down and started digging a hole in the soft earth with her hands.

"Wait, we can't do this yet," Saundra said.

"Why not?" Kelly asked.

"Because, the others aren't here yet."

Saundra thought about the others one at a time. When she felt them like she had before, she pulled them into the kingdom.

Walking over a small rise with his green cloak and a new walking stick carved from a very old piece of wood, Max joined them. He looked a little upset, but the world that was surrounding them was fresh and new. It quickly took his mind off of his loss. Each time he seemed to drift off in thought, he would stroke the strong wood, grin, and return his focus to what was happening around him.

"Thanks, Saundra. I needed a break," he said when he joined them.

Up from a nearby glen walked Nancy in the shiniest suit of armor any of them had ever seen. With the sun glinting off of her visor, she strode over and stood between Kelly and their mother. She lifted the visor to expose her face, and a large smile beamed from within the helm.

Her mother looked over at her as if to ask, Well, is that it? She nodded her head and her mother knelt back down and started digging. They all joined her on their knees.

Large chunks of the soft earth moved with each hand that dug into it. Like giant excavating equipment, they dug a massive hole. When they were three stories deep in the solid earth, they excavated a small hole about the size of a chest. Kelly wiggled her pen, and stone lined the small hole and filled the entire foundation they had dug out.

"Here we will place the horn and the key," Saundra said to them all. "It will serve as the foundation of our kingdom. Unless the very kingdom falls it will never be retrieved."

With her words complete and Kelly's quill continuing to inscribe the book, they all placed the key and horn into the stone-lined hole. With a flash of light the floor closed over the magical prize at the heart of the new kingdom. A gold inlaid glyph appeared on the floor over what had been the hole. There were no seams to give away the storehouse beneath it. The powerful magic trapped in the glyph would destroy whatever came to take the horn.

From the stone foundation they had cut into the land, a stone tower rose around them. Stairs formed in a spiral, rising from the edges of the glyph. Walls grew up around the staircase, and enormous metal doors closed out access to the glyph. Large pipes appeared above their heads and exited the room in several directions.

Saundra motioned to everyone to head up the stairs. When they passed through the first metal gateway, water rushed in from the surrounding stream through smaller holes in the walls. The glyph flashed as the water poured into the room and turned the first water to reach it into steam. The steam rose to the ceiling and filled the pipes that left the chamber.

The metal door closed behind them as the steam pressure activated it. Saundra and Kelly nodded to each other and then looked to Max and Nancy. Satisfied with the foundation, they climbed up to the main floor.

This tower was ten times the size of the tower the Guardian had manned. The central staircase was fully enclosed in heavy stone, and the steam pipes from the core rose to the height of the tower along its heavily defended center. At the top of each floor a network of pipes exited the core and fed wall defenses manned by steam-powered armored guards. At the lowest level steam-powered scorpion ballista fired out through sealed slits. As the tower rose above them, more powerful steam-powered siege engines with longer range would cover the farther reaches of the tower's watch. Max smiled at the upgrade in honor of his grandfather. Nancy nodded, impressed with the central defenses of their new kingdom.

"The glyph controls the steam and the guardians. None, other than the four of us, can enter this tower," Saundra explained. "If we ever need to assign others to guard this kingdom we can give them access, but the ultimate guardian is the glyph. It will decide the purity of any who stands to defend this kingdom."

With a sweep of the quill in Kelly's hand each of the three guardians that represented the branches assigned to defend the kingdom were marked. A darker green glyph, similar but distinctive for his branch, appeared on Max's robe. A coat of arms, also similar to the glyph but stylized for her duties, appeared on Nancy's shield and the circular covers that connected her pauldrons to her breastplate. A chain necklace and broach appeared on Saundra's neck. The symbol on the broach was almost a pure version of the glyph since it was her magical arm of the defenses of the kingdom that had placed the glyph.

"We are sworn to protect this kingdom and honor the kingdom it grew from. Each of us will have our own region, and the castle of the queen will oversee us all," Saundra continued.

"And, who is to be the queen?" Nancy asked. Saundra sensed a little jealousy in her question, but she ignored it. Max nodded his agreement that a decision needed to be made.

Saundra's mother stepped into the group and answered for them, "The old kingdom's queen was the one who wrote the tales. That, as you can see, will be Kelly." A crown appeared in her mother's hand, and she placed it atop Kelly's head. Saundra braced for a reaction from the others that never came. Everyone accepted the new queen. Saundra assumed it was for the same reason she accepted her sister as the queen; Kelly would be fair. Saundra's other reason was selfish. She would much prefer enjoying the kingdom, instead of toiling over the legends that would make it endure.

"I have now passed the crown to the next queen," their mother said as she turned to leave them. "My generation has passed their kingdom on to you. You are already beyond what we accomplished. Keep building this interesting world. I look forward to the tales to come." She winked at Kelly and then walked away, leaving the new guardians to their duties.

"Well, what now?" Max asked.

"Now that we have the foundation of our kingdom, we will build the tales that make it what it is," Kelly answered as she continued to write into the air.

Saundra nodded at her sister's words, but she kept her own opinion to herself. She still struggled with the kingdom that was on the other side of the door in her own room. With a passing inner giggle she decided to name it Saundra's Door.

The others shared stories and ideas that were going to make this kingdom strong, but Saundra was not ready to surrender completely to the dragon on the other side. She could not shake her concern that letting the dragon survive in the old kingdom would threaten their new kingdom.

She found herself alone after the others had walked back out into the air of the kingdom that had changed even as they watched the tower grow from its heart. She rushed to join them and marvel at what all had changed. A castle, the new Queen's castle, had appeared in the distance to the north. In each of the three remaining cardinal directions another tower rose from the valley against the protective walls of the mountains that had now moved off even farther toward the horizon. Saundra could see her own tower where they had entered the kingdom growing smaller as it receded from view. She knew she would find her magic, her mirror, and her door in that tower. She suddenly longed to be back in her simple room.

"What's on your mind?" Max asked, surprising her. Kelly and Nancy were discussing the formation of her knights. Kelly was enthralled by the romantic troops she could see living in the western tower Nancy would maintain.

She paused for a moment before answering. She was not sure if she wanted to share her concerns with anyone else, but Max had been beside her through all of the challenges up to now. She surrendered her concern and answered his question. "The door. The old kingdom."

"What about it?"

"We lost."

"Did we?"

"The dragon has the old kingdom. It won."

"Not if we don't surrender to it. The old kingdom is the seed of this one. We're continuing what the queen and the Guardian wanted. We're just protecting it better."

Saundra looked back at the giant tower that was still forming in the middle of the kingdom and nodded at his statement. "But, if we leave the old kingdom alone, won't it hurt us in the long run?"

"How? It can't get in here," Max answered.

Saundra shrugged, but something was still bothering her. She was not sure how anything could get into the new kingdom through her door. Nothing knew it existed, but she couldn't shake the feeling that everything was not as perfect as they thought.

"I'm sure you're right," she said to him and turned to walk toward her tower. She needed to talk to the mirror.

"See you in school?" Max asked as she walked away.

She nodded and walked on. The magic that had created the central tower had also expanded the kingdom. It took her a while to walk all the way back to the tower and into her personal part of the kingdom. Even as she crossed the new land, it continued to grow. She worried how large it would get before it finally stopped expanding. A year before, she would not have cared. But now, she had to think about protecting this new world.

The new tower of the Arcane Yeomen was secluded in a mysterious forest exactly as it should be. As much as Saundra was prepared for, and as much as she embraced the spooky nature of her tower, she couldn't shake the foreboding feeling that had been with her since they had left the central tower.

The same steam power that had been incorporated into that tower was now part of the entire kingdom. Her tower was no exception. When she approached the massive barrier door, it sensed her. The door opened with a loud clang and hiss. She had to admit she was not sure where it had come from, but it was cool. She could see pieces of each of them in the new kingdom, but she was not sure which of her friends had contributed the steam power to the magical design.

The door closed behind her. She was finally alone in her tower. She climbed the new central staircase to the very top where her old room was now situated.

"What's wrong?" she asked the mirror as she entered the somewhat comforting confines of her room that was now filled with steam pipes that fed into large closets. She knew that beyond the doors there would be a steam-powered automaton manning some powerful automated siege engine. There was a balcony that faced in each direction from the tower. In the growing distance to the west she could just make out the peak of the Guardian's tower.

"Nothing is wrong. Why?"

"I thought there might be something. I've felt strange since we left the new guardian's tower."

"I'm still trying to reach the farthest edges of this kingdom, but I don't sense anything wrong," the mirror reassured her.

Saundra sat down at the table where the book had been and rested from her long walk. The nagging feeling that something was wrong would not leave her.

For the fifth time, she scanned the room looking at everything new and old. Her scan ended on the door.

The wood was the same. It was still bound in heavy iron, even though the heavier metal gateways of the rest of the tower covered every other doorway. It now looked very out of place in the new kingdom.

She stared at it as if there was something about it that would be wrong. Everything looked fine. She sighed her frustration into the room and glared at the door.

That was when she saw it.

She jumped up from her seat and charged the door. Her wand was in her hand as she approached it.

With her wand out, she placed her palm against the wood and pressed the door closed.

It moved less than an inch, but it was enough.

Doubt settled into her bones. It had not been open enough to clear the frame, but she could not be sure if it was enough to let something through.

"Has anything come through this door?"

"Not as long as I have watched it."

The mirror's answer was not comforting.

"You must watch this door at all times and tell me if anything comes through it."

"And, what are you thinking of doing?"

"I'm going to keep an eye on it from the other side."

Saundra gripped the handle, threw her hood over

her head, and pointed her wand through the opening as she pulled the door open just far enough to slip through, into the old kingdom.

About the Author

T.D. Raufson spent his childhood as a software engineer and project manager. Once he finally figured out what he wanted to do when he grew up, he focused on writing his favorite kind of stories and sharing them with the world. He currently lives in Tennessee with his wife and three cats while searching for time to write all of the other stories he has never been able to complete.

Connect with Me:

Follow me on Twitter:
https://twitter.com/@tdraufson

Friend me on Facebook:
https://www.facebook.com/tdraufson

Like my Facebook page:
https://www.facebook.com/pages/T-D-Raufson/194158427380784?ref=hl